She could not find the film . . .
Was it lost or stolen?

But if the film wasn't lost—and it couldn't have been, she thought grimly, going over and over it— then it had to have been stolen, and stolen while she was taking her bath.

She sat without moving, allowing the shock of this to catch up with her, and it was a very real shock, with implications that left her a little dizzy. How frightfully arrogant she'd been, she thought, dashing about taking her snapshots so openly while all the time someone on this safari didn't want to be photographed. Someone had allowed her to snap as many of them as she pleased, and then her film had been quietly taken away from her. She had been discreetly and firmly put in her place.

Score one for the assassin, she thought.

Mrs. Pollifax on Safari

Dorothy Gilman

FAWCETT CREST • NEW YORK

I would like to thank Mr. Xen Vlahakis and Ms. Jeanne Harris of the Zambia National Tourist Bureau in New York for their generous help in providing material about Zambia, none of which included the Moses Msonthi School, which is purely fictional and does not exist.

For Marjorie Bell Fritz

CHAPTER

1

It was barely eight o'clock in the morning when the telephone call came in from Algiers, but Carstairs was already at his desk high up in the CIA building in Langley, Virginia. With his left hand he switched on a tape recorder, with his right he buzzed for his assistant while he listened with narrowed eyes. At one point he interrupted, saying, "Mind repeating that?" and scribbled several words on paper. When Bishop hurried into the office the call had just been completed.

"Sorry," Bishop said breathlessly, "I was in the men's room, sir. I've missed something?"

"You have every right to be in the men's room," Carstairs told him reproachfully, "but you've missed an important call from Algiers. We may—just *may*, Bishop

—have the first whisper of a breakthrough on the Aristotle case."

"Good God," said Bishop, staring at him incredulously. "After all these months?"

"It's possible. Remember that fabric shop that Davis' department placed under surveillance in Algiers? The stolen bank-note job," he added helpfully. "Bennet photographed some messages that were left out on a desk overnight and he decided, bless him, that one of them would interest us very much. Bright lad, Bennet. The cables and memos were in French and Arabic and he's only just finished translating them." Carstairs reached over and turned on the tape recorder. "Here we are," he said, and accelerating and then slowing the machine, he signaled to Bishop to take the words down in shorthand.

They both listened carefully as Bennet's clipped voice told them, "The original message, translated from the French, reads as follows: CONFIRM ORDER SEVENTY YARDS BLACK ARISTOTLE SILKS TO ZAMBIA THREE BOLTS COTTON DUE KAFUE PARK TWO BOLTS CHUNGA MUSLIN TEN YARDS FIVE-DAY SAFARI DESIGN CHINTZ DELIVERABLE JUNE NINE REPEAT CONFIRM RE-CONFIRM. CHABO."

"Right," said Bishop, puzzled. "Any more?"

"Yes, if you've got that down." Carstairs pressed the button and the voice resumed . . . "and when the clutter words have been extracted from the fabric order, using their usual decoding technique, the message becomes: CONFIRM ARISTOTLE TO ZAMBIA DUE KAFUE PARK CHUNGA FIVE-DAY SAFARI ON JUNE NINE REPEAT CONFIRM RE-CONFIRM. CHABO."

"Beautiful," said Bishop with feeling.

"I rather like it myself," said Carstairs. "Very promising indeed."

"Aristotle," Bishop mused, and shook his head. "I'd really begun to believe the man invisible, you know. All these assassinations and no one's ever noticed him in the crowd or come up with a description. How does he do it? It took us four months just to learn he has a code name and he's still a faceless, nameless Mr. X."

"He may have the reputation of being invisible," said Carstairs, "but damn it he's not supernatural." He pulled an atlas and a pile of maps from his desk drawer and began sorting through them. "Eventually *somebody's* had to refer to him through channels accessible to us, and it's possible that finally, at long last—" He pushed aside the atlas and began on the maps. "Here we are," he said abruptly. "Take a look at this. Central Africa in detail."

The two men bent over the map of Zambia and Carstairs pointed. "There's Kafue National Park, twenty-two thousand five hundred square kilometers in size, six hundred varieties of game. Note the names of the safari camps."

Bishop read aloud, "Ngomo, Moshi, Kafwala and Chunga." He glanced at Bennet's message and nodded. "*Due Kafue Park Chunga* . . . Chunga camp, that would mean. I must say it's a rare day when something falls this neatly into our laps."

"It hasn't yet," Carstairs reminded him, "but it's certainly an exhilarating possibility." He leaned back in his chair, his face thoughtful. "We do know a few things about our mysterious Aristotle. We know first of all that he's a mercenary, up for hire to whoever bids the highest price . . . Look at his record: Malaga was a Liberal in

Costa Rican politics, and Messague in France was a Communist. There was that British chap—Hastings, wasn't it?—who was making some headway in Ireland on negotiations when he was assassinated, and the colonel in Peru whose politics were strictly middle-of-the-road, and then of course there was Pete." His fact tightened. "Our agents may be fair game these days, but no man deserves to be shot as he walks out of church with a bride on his arm."

"No, sir," said Bishop. "However, there's just one point—"

"Something bothering you?"

Bishop was frowning. "Very much so, now that I've caught my breath. What I mean is, a safari? An assassin going on *safari*?"

"We also know," continued Carstairs, appearing to ignore this, "that Aristotle is intelligent, he has a strong instinct for survival, and he's a complete loner or someone would have talked long ago. Tell me, Bishop," he said, leaning forward and pointing a pencil at him, "if you were Aristotle, how would you negotiate your assignments? How would you make contact with your next employer?"

"How would I—" Bishop was silent, considering this. "Russian teahouse?" he said at last, flippantly. "Turkish bath? A funicular railway in the Swiss Alps? I see your point, sir. Tricky. Very, very tricky, and probably a hell of a lot more dangerous for him than actually shooting down politicians."

"Exactly. It's this touch that encourages me very much. Damned clever idea, choosing a safari, it's perfect for a rendezvous. He'd have the chance to look over his potential employer before identifying himself, and then it gives them both plenty of leisure to haggle over terms and price. He'd be far removed from cities, with access to a wide area in case negotiations blow up, and what better protective cover than a small group moving through remote bush country? The man definitely has a flair for the artistic."

"You sound as if you're painting a portrait."

"One has to," Carstairs pointed out, "and then crawl inside it and puzzle out what he'll do next, and at that stage you've pretty well got your man, Bishop."

"Do we share this with Interpol?"

Carstairs shook his head. "No, definitely not. We first insert one of our own people into that safari. If we can pin down this man, find out what he looks like, identify him, learn where he comes from——"

"Not catch him?" said Bishop, startled.

Carstairs looked amused. "My dear Bishop, would you have us ask the Republic of Zambia to arrest everyone on next Monday's safari? And on what charge? Uh-uh. This calls for the purest kind of old-fashioned intelligence-gathering, and don't underestimate it."

"I never have, sir," Bishop said meekly.

"In fact, if you consider the world's population at this given moment," pointed out Carstairs, "you can understand how it narrows the field if Aristotle turns up at Kafue Park next Monday and we capture photographs of everyone on the safari. Instead of looking for a needle in a haystack, we'll have pictures of perhaps a dozen people to sort through, identify, trace and verify. Exposure does wonders for invisible men," he added dryly, "and Interpol can take it from there. What's the date today?"

"June first."

Carstairs nodded. "We've got to move fast, then. We've barely time to find the right agent and get him over there. Set up the computer, Bishop, will you? We'll run through the possibilities."

"It'll only take a minute, sir." Bishop walked over to the closet where the machine they referred to as the Monster was housed. He punched MASTER LIST, fiddled with knobs, fed it classifications like *Africa*, *Zambia* and *Tourist* and called to his superior. "Here you are, sir. Beginning with A, right down to Z."

"Always reminds me of a damn slot machine," growled Carstairs, gazing up at the screen with its myriads of blinking lights, and then he said, "John Sebastian Farrell! What the hell's he doing on this list when he hasn't worked for us in three years?"

Bishop, who had a memory to equal any computer, said, "Hmmm . . . Well, I could hazard a guess, sir. In that letter of resignation he sent us three years ago from South America—scrawled, if I remember correctly, on a torn sheet of wrapping paper—he said he was off to Africa to reclaim his soul or some such thing, and we could send any sums owed him to Farrell, care of Barclay's Bank, Lusaka, Zambia."

Carstairs frowned. "Something about cleaner air and a cleaner life, wasn't it? That still doesn't explain what he's doing on the computer list."

"A mistake, I think." Bishop left the computer, went to the phone, dialed a number and rattled questions into it. When he hung up he looked pleased. "Called Bookkeeping, sir. They tell me they've been regularly mailing Farrell's pension checks to Zambia for three years, and apparently that's what the computer picked up.

They're terribly sorry and his name is being removed at once."

"He's still there? Those checks are being cashed?"

"That's what they tell me."

"Farrell," said Carstairs musingly, and returned to his desk and sat down. "Damn it, Bishop," he said, scowling, "I've known Farrell since OSS days, he worked for this department for fifteen years, yet why is it I can no longer think of Farrell without thinking of Emily Pollifax?"

Bishop laughed. "That was her first assignment, wasn't it? After she'd turned up in Mason's office to naïvely apply for work as a spy? And you'd been looking for a cozy grandmotherly type for your courier job and you took her on, and when all hell broke loose you thought—"

"I know what I thought," Carstairs said, cutting him off, and suddenly grinned. "Do you remember, Bishop? When it was all over they sat right here in this office. Farrell was in bandages, looking like death itself, and Mrs. Pollifax was in that damn Albanian goatherder's outfit . . . they'd just been pulled out of the Adriatic and I'd given her up for dead, I'd given them both up for dead—and she sat here pulling rabbits out of a hat—"

"Out of her petticoats, wasn't it?" said Bishop, smiling.

"—and it turned out that a complete amateur had duped all the professionals." He stopped smiling and said abruptly, "Mrs. Pollifax, of course."

Bishop, reading his mind, was shocked. "Tangling with a cold-blooded assassin, sir?"

"She's tangled with them before," pointed out Carstairs, "but this time she doesn't have to tangle with anyone at all, just take photographs. Most of these safaris nowadays are camera-shooting, not hunting safaris, and there'll be cameras in everybody's pocket."

"Maybe," said Bishop grudgingly, and then, smiling, "Of course she'd be marvelous at it. Ingenuous, artless, the sort everyone confides in . . . Do you think Aristotle might confide in her, too?"

Carstairs gave him a sour glance. "Try not to be naïve, Bishop," and then as his gaze moved to the clock, "She'll need a yellow-fever shot and someone will have to pull some strings to get her a visa in a hurry, and if that safari's booked solid there'll have to be more strings pulled, although thank heaven it's early June and not the high season yet in Africa. Bishop—"

Bishop sighed. "New York, I suppose?"

"Right. Get the first plane over and start things moving. The Zambia National Tourist Bureau's on Fifty-eighth Street, I think, and so is the embassy that will produce the visa. While you're phoning about a plane reservation I'll call Mrs. Pollifax and see if she can take this on. God, let's hope so," he said fervently. "After your business in New York you can go on to New Jersey and brief her."

"Right. Oh, by the way," said Bishop, pausing at the door. "If she's available do I mention Farrell being in Zambia?"

Carstairs considered this judiciously. "You'd better, I suppose, just in case—heaven forbid—they accidentally bump into each other at the wrong time. It could give the whole show away." He hesitated and then added, "Hold on a moment." Smiling almost mischievously, he said, "I'll go even further. Ask her to give Farrell a ring on the telephone when she arrives in Lusaka. He must be in the book. There might not be time for a reunion before her safari, but they could certainly get together afterward."

Bishop looked at him curiously. "That's a bit unusual, isn't it?"

"Highly irregular but also crafty," admitted Carstairs. "I'd like to know how our old friend Farrell is doing. Damn it, Bishop, I miss that man," he said indignantly. "I can name half a dozen jobs in the past three years he would have done a hell of a lot better than anyone else. He must be bored to death with retirement."

"It's possible," said Bishop.

"Of course it's possible. Definitely get her to Lusaka early, Bishop, and ask her to look him up before she flutters about photographing everyone on safari. Now go away and let me tackle Mrs. Pollifax before she slips through our fingers. . . ."

At that particular moment Mrs. Pollifax was standing in the middle of her living room practicing the karate on-guard stance. One could never be too prepared, she thought, adjusting her balance so that her weight was placed equally on both feet, and when this had been accomplished she curled each hand into a fist and attempted a quick horizontal slash. More than this she dared not risk. Lorvale, her instructor, was currently enthusiastic about attacking with blood-curdling shouts of *"Ki-ya!"* but it seemed reasonable to suppose that this would bring her neighbors down upon her head.

The telephone began ringing and Mrs. Pollifax reluctantly disengaged her stance to answer it. She could tell at once from the rustling sounds in the background that the call was long distance. A muffled voice said, "Hold please," and then a familiar one said, "Carstairs here. Mrs. Pollifax, could you leave for Africa this weekend?"

Mrs. Pollifax reflected that karate did help; this somewhat startling query did not unbalance her at all. "Yes, I think I could," she told him. "How *are* you, Mr. Carstairs?"

"Understaffed and terribly busy," he snapped. "You did say yes?"

"It slipped out," she said, "but if I can find someone to water my geraniums, yes I could go to Africa this weekend."

"Then start looking," he said, his voice a shade less harassed. "Although not for a few hours, because Bishop's on his way to New York, or will be in a few minutes. He'll make all the arrangements for you. Who's your doctor?"

Startled, she told him.

"Good. Bishop will be around to see you. Sometime between one and two o'clock?"

"Either will be fine," she told him, hung up and at once felt a shock tremor move inch by inch down her spine to her toes. *What* had possessed her to say yes? She couldn't possibly leave for Africa this weekend, the idea was preposterous. Africa was halfway around the world and one prepared cautiously for such a trip, announcing it to friends, reading guidebooks, making lists in advance. That was how her neighbor Miss Hartshorne traveled, and at the moment it appeared to Mrs. Pollifax a very luxurious and sane way to do such things.

On the other hand, she could remember feeling exactly this way at other times when her tranquil world had collided with Carstairs' rough and dangerous world, and acknowledging this she let her mind run back over past adventures. She was, miraculously, still alive and sound, with dimensions added to her life that brought a chuckle at rare moments, such as when the garden club had shown a prize-winning Colin Ramsey film on Turkey and she had recognized two of the women in baggy pants and veils drawing water from a well. This time it was to be Africa.

She said it aloud—"Africa"—and at the sound of the word her heart began to beat faster and she realized that she was smiling. Africa, the dark continent. Tarzan. She remembered that when her son Roger was a boy she had taken him to see every Tarzan film that came to the Rivoli theater, and when his tastes had begun to veer toward Rita Hayworth she had gone to see Tarzan alone, enchanted by the animals, the steamy jungles, poisoned arrows and roar of lions . . . Lions, she thought with a gasp. Even if Carstairs sent her to a bustling African city she must find a way to see lions. She would *demand* lions.

How dull her life had been growing lately, she thought, and how exciting to realize that she was going to see Africa. There suddenly seemed a great many things to do. She would have to sort through her entire collection of *National Geographics*, and there was all that material on game conservation in her desk drawer . . .

With a guilty start she realized that it was nine o'clock and the breakfast dishes were still unwashed. Bishop would be coming in a few hours too, and she wondered if he was still partial to chocolate eclairs—she would have to visit Mr. Omelianuk's delicatessen at once. She reached for her coat, tucked her hair under a floppy straw hat, and went out.

It was a brilliant June morning but she walked carefully nevertheless, for the ground beneath her might be covered over with cement, and her eyes shaded by straw, but in Mrs. Pollifax's mind she wore a cork helmet and moved soundlessly through tall grasses, her ears alert for the sound of native drums.

CHAPTER

2

Bishop arrived precisely at two o'clock, and although he looked harassed he had lost none of his insouciance, which, considering the years he'd spent as Carstairs' assistant, always astonished Mrs. Pollifax. "Why don't you look older?" she protested, taking his coat. "You never do, it's disconcerting."

"Nor do you," he told her gallantly, giving her a kiss on the cheek, "but in my case I *know* I'm older because my pushups are growing lazier and when Carstairs loses his temper at me I sometimes feel an overwhelming urge to cry. Is that for me?" he asked, staring fascinated at the table in the living room set with damask linen, china teapot, flowered Haviland cups and pastries.

"*Especially* for you. Sit down and I'll pour. There are five eclairs."

"I count six."

"One," she told him reproachfully, "is for me. I suppose you're understaffed and overworked because of last year's congressional investigations? Which, I must add, was very shocking indeed. Even *you* need some checks and balances, you know."

"*We* are not and were not being investigated," he said, sitting down and picking up an eclair. "Carstairs asked me to tell you very firmly that his department has remained scrupulous to the letter in all its undertakings." He hesitated and then said dryly, "At least as scrupulous as can be expected when our business is to gather information by nefarious means, hit troublesome people over the head, and indulge in other interesting forms of skulduggery."

Mrs. Pollifax, recalling certain people that she herself had been forced to hit over the head, did not comment: it was a very modest number, of course, but one of which she was sure neither her garden club nor her pastor would approve. She continued pouring tea, noticing that Bishop was already devouring his second eclair. "You've not had lunch?"

"Clever of you to guess," he said, swallowing. "Carstairs packed me off at eight forty-five with a thousand errands to do, and presently you'll have your share to do too. I don't suppose he told you anything?"

"Not a thing, except it's Africa."

"He wants you to go on safari."

"On safari!" Mrs. Pollifax stared at him in astonishment. "*Safari?*" she repeated incredulously.

Bishop watched her eyes subtly shift focus as if she gazed at something unseen to him and very far away. She looked, in fact, as if she were experiencing a beatific vision, and understanding the processes of her mind, he shook his head. "No, Mrs. Pollifax," he said firmly, "they don't wear cork helmets in Africa any more."

She forgave him this underhanded remark but not without an indignant glance. She said with dignity, "I would be *delighted* to go on safari, cork hat or no. But why? Surely there's more?"

"Naturally. It's a very specific safari starting out next Monday in Kafue National Park in Zambia. That's in Central Africa, and if you're not up on your African countries, it was called Northern Rhodesia before it gained its independence in 1964. You can read all about it because I've brought you lots of pamphlets. It's good safari country, not as well-known, perhaps, as Kenya or Tanzania just to the north, but it's rapidly getting discovered. Less touristy, more relaxed and unspoiled . . . Actually, Kafue Park is one of the larger game parks in the world—half the size of Switzerland—and of course the Victoria Falls are in Zambia too."

"Of course," said Mrs. Pollifax, "and the President of Zambia, Kenneth Kaunda, recently visited Washington."

He looked impressed. "I'd forgotten that. Well, we'd like you to hurry over there, join the safari, get acquainted with your companions and take pictures of them—every one of them—either openly or surreptitiously."

"Is that all?" asked Mrs. Pollifax, puzzled.

"Believe me, it's frightfully important," he told her. "We want everyone on safari observed and recorded, and for this we need someone who has always dreamed of a safari, someone utterly charmed by a lioness in the bush, fond of birds and flowers, and of course given to compulsive picture-taking. In fact," he said with a smile,

"I'd urge you to carry along a stupefying number of snapshots of your grandchildren, and if you don't have any, rent some. You know how to operate a camera?"

She nodded, and he slit open the mysterious package he'd brought with him. "Here's a very good normal camera," he said, handing it over to her. "Nothing fancy, you can buy it in any drugstore, easy to operate, small enough to tuck into your pocket. And here," he added, bringing out a jeweler's box, "is a different sort of camera, in case one of the group is camera-shy."

"This is a camera?" said Mrs. Pollifax opening the box and staring at a brooch inside. "It can't be, surely."

"A bit vulgar, isn't it?" he said cheerfully. "But you have to admit it doesn't look like a camera."

"It certainly doesn't." She lifted the lapel pin out of the box and examined it. It had been designed as a miniature clock with a pendulum, its total length about three inches, which included the pendulum from which hung two small gold balls. The face was a sunflower with gold petals surrounding it, and two glittering eyes were set into the center with a curved smile below them.

"Lacks only a cuckoo," pointed out Bishop. "You pull on the chain to take a snapshot. Just a slight tug will do it, and then you touch the hands of the clock to move the film along for the next shot. The lenses are in the eyes. Takes forty snapshots, and then you bring it back to us and we smash it and remove the film."

"Very ingenious," murmured Mrs. Pollifax, and then with a thoughtful glance, "Just who is going to be on this safari, Bishop?"

"It's purest intelligence-gathering," he assured her blithely. "Someone of interest to us may be popping up there. You know how it is, a rumor, a whisper . . . all in the name of the game."

Mrs. Pollifax's smile was gentle. "I've never heard you lean so heavily on clichés before, Bishop. In the name of the *game*?"

"Well, I can't tell you *much* more," he said candidly, "because Carstairs won't allow it. But it won't hurt to point out that there have been a number of assassinations in the past seven months that have never been solved. The most publicized were Malaga in Costa Rica and Messague in France."

She nodded.

"According to the particular netherworld we're in touch with—made up of criminals, spies, informants and hangers-on—they were accomplished by one man with the code name of Aristotle. We don't know anything more about him but we've intercepted a message leading us to believe he'll be on this safari Monday, and that's all I can tell you." He brightened. "But I *can* tell you what the computer announced this morning when we fed it a list of possibilities for the job. It seems an old friend of yours is in Zambia. He doesn't work for us any more but you know him very well."

"I do?"

Bishop grinned. "I'd assume that after sharing a cell together in Albania for two weeks you'd know each other pretty damn well."

"Farrell?" gasped Mrs. Pollifax. "John Sebastian Farrell?"

"None other."

"But what's he doing in Zambia, and why doesn't he work for you any longer?"

"We haven't the foggiest idea what he's doing in Zambia," said Bishop, "and he isn't working for us any more because he resigned three years ago. All we know is that his pension—"

"His what?"

"We do pay pensions," Bishop said, amused by the look on her face, "and his payments are being sent to Farrell in care of Barclay's Bank, Lusaka, Zambia. Better make a note of that. Carstairs suggests you look him up when you get to Lusaka and see if he's missing us as much as we've missed him. He should be in the phone book if he's settled down."

"Farrell," said Mrs. Pollifax, her eyes shining. "That dear man. A scoundrel, of course, but I'd trust him with my life, you know. Although not," she added thoughtfully, "with my daughter. No, definitely not with my daughter."

"Mothers always trust me with their daughters," Bishop said wistfully, and then, pulling himself together, unzipped his attaché case. "There's a lot to be done," he said briskly. "I've already visited the Zambia National Tourist Bureau today, as well as the Zambian Embassy. Mercifully, the tourist bureau has room for you in next Monday's safari. Kafue Park is opening only this week—the rainy season's just ended, you see—so luck was with us. As for your visa, it took persuasion, but if you'll let me carry your passport back to New York with me this afternoon they'll issue you one immediately and return your passport to you by special delivery. That leaves your yellow-fever vaccination. Your doctor is being sent the vaccine and you're to see him at four o'clock tomorrow afternoon. You leave Saturday night for London, and

Sunday night for Lusaka, and here are your plane tickets,"
he said, placing them on the table. "Here are also book-
lets and pamphlets and brochures about Zambia—" He
placed these on the growing pile and glanced up at her.
"Are you still with me? Am I forgetting something?"

"Clothes," pointed out Mrs. Pollifax.

Bishop understood at once; it was why mothers trusted
him. "Go to New York early on Saturday before your
plane leaves, if you can't make it sooner. Slacks, a bush
jacket, a sweater, good walking shoes . . . Abercrombie's
will be just the place for you. And oh yes, here are anti-
malarial tablets, good God I almost forgot them. Start
taking them at *once*." He glanced at his watch and sighed.
"I hope that's all because damn it I'm already an hour
behind schedule and I've got to be running along."

"Oh Bishop, so soon?"

He nodded. "It's one of the deficiencies of my life with
Carstairs that I never see anyone for more than half an
hour, and always on the run. Beautiful chocolate eclairs,"
he said fervently. "All five of them." Collecting his attaché
case, he arose. "Now I need your passport."

She found it in the desk drawer and gave it to him.
"I'll send you a postcard from Zambia," she told him.

"Better not," he said regretfully. "Just take lots of
snapshots for us—of everyone on that safari, barring
no one—and have your reunion with Farrell and see if
he's bored yet. He called you the Duchess, didn't he?"

"It seems a century ago," admitted Mrs. Pollifax, following him to the door. "Do you remember how naïve I
used to be?"

"No, really?" said Bishop, amused. "Yes . . . Well, I
don't find you particularly hardened even now, but there's

always hope, isn't there? Don't forget that yellow-fever
shot tomorrow and stay out of trouble, you hear?"

"Of course," she told him, and watched him hurry down
the hall to the elevator. When he had disappeared she
closed the door, walked back into the living room, and
remembering how her morning had begun, she nostal-
gically assumed the karate on-guard stance again. So
much had changed, however—even to the slant of the sun
through the windows—that as she cut the air with a horizontal slash she tried a small and daring *"Ki-ya."* This
proved unsatisfying. Drawing a deeper breath she braced
herself and shouted triumphantly, *"KI-YA!"*

CHAPTER

3

On Saturday Mrs. Pollifax left early for New York to spend an afternoon at Abercrombie's before her plane departure. She was already flushed with triumph at finding a new hat for traveling. It was not precisely a cork helmet but it looked so remarkably like one that she no longer felt deprived. It was a bulbous white straw with a single red feather that began in the back and ran up and across the top of the crown and down to the tiny brim in front, where it was held in place by a clip. The narrow line of scarlet relieved the hat's austerity and added a dashing touch to her two-year-old blue-and-white-striped suit.

Nothing had prepared her for Abercrombie's, however. It was true that she had once or twice poked her head in the door out of curiosity, but she had never before entered the store with purpose, or with a safari waiting in the wings. Now, given *carte blanche*, she lost all inhibition, especially after discovering that the five pounds she'd lost during the winter placed her unexpectedly in a pair of size 12 slacks. In only half an hour she dealt with her wardrobe: two pairs of khaki slacks went into her suitcase, a trim bush jacket, a heavy turtleneck sweater, and a long pale-blue cardigan with a sash. Her remaining creativeness she saved for Abercrombie's accessories, which left her in a state of ecstasy. She succumbed immediately to a pair of enormous tinted round sungoggles which gave her the look of a Martian; she found herself wondering how she could have survived for so long without them. She bought a flashlight and then a pencil flashlight. Regretfully she decided against a set of aluminum dishes that folded one inside of another until they fitted into a small pouch. She bought a dust veil because there was always the chance that she might be caught in a dust storm; she added a silk kerchief with zebras racing across it, and believed that she had concluded her purchases until she saw the umbrella.

"It's rather large," the clerk pointed out, watching her with a fascinated eye.

"Yes, but isn't it beautiful?" she said in an awed voice, admiring its rainbow effect of scarlets, yellows, blues, pinks and oranges.

"I believe the rainy season has ended in Zambia."

"True," she said reflectively, "but then it's really a matter of semantics, don't you think?"

"I beg your pardon?" he said, startled by the *non sequitur*.

"I mean that an umbrella could just as easily be called

a parasol, don't you think? If the rainy season's over there'll be sun. A great deal of sun, I should imagine."

"Yes," said the young man, intrigued. "Yes, that's certainly true. Sun and dust."

She nodded. "And I shall have my dust veil and a parasol."

"Yes you will," he said, beginning to follow her line of reasoning.

"And then if one falls in love with something," she confessed, "one is always sorry later one didn't buy it."

"Exactly," he said warmly. "Of course you must have it then."

Mrs. Pollifax agreed, and bought it, and was not even sorry when the airline classified it as a weapon and she had to watch it dropped down baggage chutes all during her trip. It was, she thought, a very minor inconvenience when it was such a glorious umbrella. Or parasol.

And so at ten o'clock that evening Mrs. Pollifax set out on her flight to London, suitably vaccinated and carrying her suitcase full of drip-dries, khaki and other small treasures. Not for her the luxury of magazines: once in flight she efficiently brought out her book on Central Africa animals and read, "The roan antelope is, in general color, a pale reddish brown, slightly darker on the hind quarters, the hair short and coarse," and then she fell asleep. Upon waking she read, "The sable antelope is rich deep brown, the old males jet black," and fell asleep again. At Heathrow airport she napped for a few hours in a day room, and at eight o'clock in the evening she boarded the Zambia Airways plane and resumed her trip to Lusaka.

Here she met with her first disappointment. Since

Zambia was a new country, roughly a decade old and developing fast—the Third World, she thought solemnly—she had expected a few exotic companions on her flight, but instead she appeared to be surrounded by British families on holiday with babies and small children. The only bright notes provided were the lovely black stewardesses in their orange minidresses.

Mrs. Pollifax dozed and woke, determined not to miss her first glimpse of Africa. Very early in the morning, at first light, she opened her eyes and looked out over a floor of wrinkled clouds to see a bright-orange sun slip out of the dusk and trail a line of soft pink behind it. All drowsiness vanished as she sat up in anticipation. Gradually the clouds brightened and dispersed, the sun shed a warm clear light over the sky, and Mrs. Pollifax, looking down from the plane, saw Africa.

Africa at last, and not a dark continent at all, she thought exuberantly, staring at the strange world below. From this height it looked as if the earth's skin had been peeled back and cooked into a dull-orange crust and then lightly sprinkled with green lichen. Oddest of all were the upheavals appearing here and there in the earth. Really, she thought, they looked just like bubbles in a thick stew on the stove.

Soon the view grew softer, and the pale dusty green turned into rich chenille, defined by narrow red-clay roads like seams in a garment stretching to the horizon. Once she leaned forward, certain that she saw a village of huts below, and it thrilled her to think of natives waking to the dawn without realizing that she saw them from the sky. She began to grow excited about landing on this earth spread out below her, she began to consider what lay ahead . . . In her purse she carried vouchers sent her by the tourist bureau in New York, and she recalled that she was to be met at the airport by a tourist guide and whisked off to the hotel ("Transfer from Lusaka International Airport to Hotel Intercontinental: $6.60"), and she would remain in Lusaka for roughly six hours ("1430 departure Hotel Intercontinental to Chunga Safari Village, KT/3"). But before she left for Kafue Park at half-past two this afternoon she had every hope of contacting Farrell, and this gave an added fillip to her arrival.

Ever since leaving New York she had found herself wondering what Farrell might be doing in Zambia, and now she tried once again to fit what she knew of him into the rust-colored terrain below her. She remembered that when she'd first met Farrell he'd been running an art gallery in Mexico City, but he'd also been a bona fide painter himself. He'd mentioned smuggling guns to Castro in the early days of the revolution, and she knew that at one time he'd operated a charter boat out of Acapulco, and somewhere in there he'd also begun to work for Carstairs. Now he was retired.

Zambia was a land-locked country, so there would be no charter boats; its revolution had ended in 1964, so there were no guns to smuggle. What would Farrell have found here? "Perhaps an art gallery," she thought, and as she turned this over in her mind she began to like it very much. He would collect Zambian art, she decided, specializing in wood carvings, thumb-pianos and spears, which he would sell to tourists; but of course he would paint his own pictures, too, and she would buy one. Definitely she would buy one and carry it home and hang it in her apartment. She continued weaving pleasant little fantasies about his new life in Zambia, adding a beautiful wife because he would, she felt, make an excellent husband—retired rakes so often did—and perhaps there was a child by now.

She realized the *No Smoking-Fasten Seatbelts* sign had been blinking at her for some time, and now a voice interrupted her speculations to announce their imminent landing. Mrs. Pollifax tucked away her book, fastened her seatbelt and tried to discipline her excitement. This was not easy, because after two nights spent on planes the effect of her arrival on a new continent was rather like an overdose of adrenalin laced by large amounts of caffeine.

The 707 descended, taxied past a line of Zambia Airways DC-8s and came to a stop before a handsome modern terminal building. Mrs. Pollifax disembarked and immediately learned that African mornings could be cold. Shivering, she moved through Passport Controls, where she filled out a tiresome number of forms in a room hung with signs that read PRACTISE HUMANISM, and HUMANISM MUNTU UZYI BANTUIVYINA ULALEMEKA BACEMBELE. She then walked out into the waiting room to a wall of people waiting behind ropes. One of these people detached himself and moved toward her, a smiling young black man in a blue zip-up jacket tossed over a plaid shirt. "Mrs. Pollifax?"

"Yes," she said in relief.

"I'm Homer Kulumbala. Welcome to Lusaka."

"How do you do," she said, beaming at him.

They waited for her suitcase, and then for her umbrella, which appeared to startle Homer. After one look at it he said sternly, "This could be easily stolen. You must guard it carefully while in the city. It is very beautiful."

"Yes, isn't it?" she agreed happily.

A few minutes later they were speeding toward town in a VW bus emblazoned with the tourist bureau insignia. Mrs. Pollifax's first impressions were of space and newness, and a great deal of bougainvillea, and when they drew up to the hotel—which was also spacious, new and surrounded by bougainvillea—Homer told her that it was he who would be driving her to Chunga camp at half-past two, and that she would see more of the capital later, on the trip out of town. She thanked him and gave her suitcase to the porter, but the umbrella she carried herself.

As soon as Mrs. Pollifax reached her hotel room she did not stop to relax; she paused only long enough to extract her striped flannel pajamas from her suitcase and then she reached for the telephone directory on the shelf under the phone. Sitting down on the bed with the book on her lap—she was surprised to see by its cover that it encompassed the entire country—she eagerly turned the pages until she found Lusaka.

"A . . . B . . . C . . . D . . . E . . . F," she murmured, and running a finger down the list of F's she ticked off Farmer's Co-operative Society of Zambia Ltd., Farmers Prime Butchery, Farmers Produce Association, Fashion Mart Ltd. . . . the name of Farrell was conspicuously missing.

Impossible, she thought, frowning, and resolutely began again, attributing the oversight to tiredness: Farmer's Cooperative Society of Zambia Ltd., Farmers Prime Butchery . . .

There was no Farrell listed among the F's.

Thoroughly frustrated now, she began thumbing through pages at random, checking out F's in towns with names like Chingold, Kazimuli, Kitwe, Kabwe. There seemed to be very few family names listed, and a vast number of government offices and co-ops. In small towns with only a dozen or so entries she noticed that telephone service was available for only a few hours each day, but none of these listed a Farrell either. Extensive research lay ahead, and she realized that in only six and a half hours she would be leaving for Chunga.

This time she began at the very beginning of the directory, but after an hour's diligent study she had still found no John Sebastian Farrell. Yet Bishop had reported that he was *here*, and that all of the checks sent to him in Lusaka had been picked up and cashed.

Barclay's Bank, she thought abruptly and, reaching for the telephone, dialed the front desk to ask what hours the banks were open. From eight o'clock to twelve, the desk clerk informed her.

It was half-past eight now. "And the afternoon hours?"

There were no afternoon hours.

Mrs. Pollifax thanked him, and with a wistful glance at her pajamas she picked up her purse and went out.

Cairo Road was a bustling main street lined with modern shops. A strip of green divided its double roadway, and there were pleasing, tree-lined cobbled spaces inserted between the buildings, restful to the eye. Women in long bright skirts, blouses and turbans mingled with women in smart frocks and sandals. Almost all of the faces were black, and almost all of the voices she overheard had unexpected and very charming British accents.

It was a noisy, cheerful scene, with a great deal of tooting from the small cars, motor scooters, Land Rovers and bicycles that streamed up and down Cairo Road.

Mrs. Pollifax paid her driver and walked into Barclay's Bank to the window marked INQUIRIES—MAIL. The man behind the counter looked forbidding, his black face buttoned into bureaucratic aloofness. She cleared her throat to gain his attention. "This is where mail is picked up?"

"Yes, madam," he said, regarding her with expressionless eyes. "Your name is—?"

She shook her head. "I'm not looking for mail, I'm looking for a man who receives his mail here. For three years his mail has been directed to him in care of Barclay's Bank, Lusaka. I don't have his address," she explained, "and I've come all the way from America and I find he's not listed in the telephone book."

"This is rather interesting," he said politely.

"His name is John Sebastian Farrell," she told him. "I thought perhaps after three years you might be forwarding his letters to an address?"

His gaze remained aloof, but after a moment he turned and called, "Jacob?"

The beaming young man who appeared was of a different generation; his tie was flaming red and his face eager. Mrs. Pollifax repeated her query to him, and he promptly said, "No address, he still gets his mail here."

"Personally?" asked his superior, who suddenly gave evidence of understanding exactly what Mrs. Pollifax wanted.

"I've never seen him," said Jacob. "A boy picks it up."

"Always?" faltered Mrs. Pollifax.

"I have never seen this man either," said the older

clerk. "There has been some curiosity about him, of course. I too have only seen a boy ask for Mr. Farrell's mail. Not often, sometimes not for three months. A different boy each time."

"Oh," said Mrs. Pollifax, her heart sinking. "Oh dear. Are there—perhaps I shouldn't ask—but are there any letters waiting for him now, so that someone might be picking up his mail soon? I could write a note," she explained.

Now they were both gripped by her problem, touched by her dismay, their eyes sympathetic. "It would be good for you to write a letter to your friend," Jacob said earnestly, ."but only two weeks ago Mr. Farrell's mail was collected. I myself gave it out—a small boy again, with the note authorizing him to gather it—"

"I see," said Mrs. Pollifax. "Yes—well, I thank you very much, both of you."

"You must write him," the older man said firmly.

"Yes," she said. "Yes, of course."

She walked outside into the sun again, crossed the road to the center strip and sat down on a bench under a tree. She felt almost inconsolable, and very close to tears, which was probably the result of two nights of spasmodic sleep, but it was also due to a sense of acute loss. It was not just that Farrell was part of her assignment, it had nothing at all to do with her assignment. She was genuinely fond of Farrell and she had anticipated seeing him.

A newspaper lay beside her on the bench and she picked it up and opened it to conceal her tears. She saw that it was this morning's *Times of Zambia*, and out of some vague hope that she might find Farrell listed in it

she turned to the back page and prepared to read the
entire paper. On this last page, however, she found
herself staring at CLASSIFIED ADVERTISEMENTS, and at a
column marked *Personals* in particular. She read:

GOOD SAMARITAN: befriend suicidal and de-
spairing. Write Box 1–A or telephone . . .

LOST: Mercedes keys left on counter National
Commercial Bank Ltd. 10:30 Monday. Finder please
return to . . .

Mrs. Pollifax turned thoughtful; she hadn't lost any car
keys but she'd lost Farrell; she wasn't suicidal, but at
the moment she felt disappointed almost to the point of
despair. She glanced at the masthead of the newspaper
and made her decision. Taking the paper with her she
retraced her steps to the bank and inquired the way to
the *Times* office. Directions were given her, and ten
minutes later she entered the *Times of Zambia* building,
only a few blocks down Cairo Road, and was given a
form to fill out.

She wrote her name and her address in the United
States, and then:

JOHN SEBASTIAN FARRELL: here for safari,
love to see you. Back June 16 Hotel Intercontinental. Duchess.

As she completed this she became aware that a man
had begun writing out a similar form across the desk
from her, and glancing up she found him staring at her.

He was a big man, several inches over six feet tall, with a seamed, deeply tanned face and a thatch of white hair. Meeting her glance he nodded. "Good face."

"I beg pardon?" she said, startled.

"Good face," he repeated in a voice that marked him as American. "Look old enough to not mind my saying so."

"Old enough, yes," she said, smiling at him.

"Lost my wallet," he explained with a huge gesture encompassing the desk, his pencil and the office.

"I've lost a friend," she said, and carried her message to the young man at the counter. "How soon can you put this in your newspaper?" she asked him.

The young man accepted her copy and annoyingly read it back to her in a loud, clear voice. " *'John Sebastian Farrell: here for safari, love to see you. Back June 16 Hotel Intercontinental. Duchess.'* " With a glance at his watch he assured her that it would be in tomorrow morning's paper without fail, and that it would cost her one *kwacha* and twenty *ngwee.*

"Roughly two dollars American," put in the huge American, waiting beside her, and peering into her change purse he pointed to one of the larger silver coins. "There's your *kwacha,* the little one's the twenty *ngwee.*"

"Yes—thank you," she stammered, gave the coins to the man and hurried toward the door. Behind her she heard the American say, "Morning. Cyrus Reed's my name. Lost a wallet."

Out on the street she found a taxi discharging a passenger at the building next door and firmly captured it. Once back in her hotel room again, she climbed into her pajamas and resolved to put all thoughts of Farrell aside for the moment. She had done all that she could; if he was still in Zambia he'd see the advertisement, and the rest would be up to him. In the meantime, she thought, animals and Aristotle lay ahead of her. Smiling, she fell asleep.

CHAPTER

4

Her alarm awoke Mrs. Pollifax at one, and she jumped out of bed and eagerly approached her suitcase. She opened it lovingly and removed the new bush jacket and the new slacks, reached for a drip-dry blue turtleneck blouse and brought out her comfortable walking shoes. There was a small delay while she fumbled with price tags, but once she was in her safari clothes the effect was dazzling: the old Emily Pollifax, vice-president of the Save-Our-Environment Committee and secretary of the New Brunswick Garden Club had vanished along with the straw hat she'd packed away in her suitcase. She looked —swashbuckling, she thought, admiring herself in the mirror, yes, definitely swashbuckling. Tarzan, she felt, would have approved.

There was a further delay while she tried on the khaki

hat, the sun-goggles, the dust veil, and unfurled her parasol, but eventually she was packed and ready to leave. She descended in the elevator, paid her bill at the desk, left her bag with the porter at the front door and, still carrying her umbrella, headed for the Coffee Hut for lunch before her departure for Chunga. She was hesitating at the door when a man's voice behind her said, "Ha— found you again. Lunching now?"

Mrs. Pollifax turned and found herself staring into a kelly-green shirt. Lifting her gaze she identified its owner as Cyrus Reed, last seen at the *Times of Zambia*. "As a matter of fact, yes."

"Good. Have it with me," he said, and taking a firm grip on her elbow he piloted her into the patio and seated her efficiently at an umbrella-shaded table. "Don't give you a chance to refuse," he said, taking the chair opposite her.

"No, you didn't."

"Don't often ask women to lunch," he said gruffly. "To dinner either, for that matter. Nuisance, that sort of thing. You aren't, I hope, a real Duchess? Couldn't help overhearing your classified advertisement in the news office."

"He did read it in a loud voice," she admitted. "Actually I'm Emily Pollifax. Duchess was a—a sort of nickname."

He extended an arm across the flowers and they gravely shook hands. He was certainly a large man; big was the only word for him, she decided, looking at him, but it seemed a matter of frame and muscle rather than fat. He moved and spoke slowly, as if stricken by lethargy, but he had whisked her to a table in seconds, and his smile, drowsy as it was, was singularly warm and responsive and his eyes shrewd. There was something very oriental about his eyes, she thought; it was because they were set into his face on the same plane as his brows, like almonds pressing into a snowman's face. Those Chinese lids increased his sleepy look and gave him the appearance of a large and slightly rumpled mandarin.

He said now, observantly, "Eyes had a faraway look when you explained the nickname. Good friend, this Farrell?"

"A very good friend, yes."

"Only kind to have," he said, nodding. "Imaginative idea, advertising. Cyrus Reed's my name, by the way. Lawyer, Connecticut. Care for a drink?"

Mrs. Pollifax smiled at the hovering waiter but shook her head. "I've not a great deal of time," she explained. "I'm being called for at half-past two."

"Then we'll order. I can recommend the chicken because I've had it every day since my arrival. Tirelessly, one might say."

Mr. Reed, it seemed, had been in Lusaka for four days. "My daughter," he explained, "is exhausting. Insisted on our stopping in Rome on the way here, and now she's gone off to Livingstone to see Victoria Falls while I catch my breath. Insisted on renting a car for the trip, said she'd see more of the country."

"I expect she will," said Mrs. Pollifax cheerfully.

"Already late returning. Due back three hours ago. What brings you here?"

"I'm leaving on safari this afternoon," she told him.

His sleepy gaze sharpened. "This afternoon? Not by any chance the five-day Kafue Park safari starting officially tomorrow morning?"

She looked at him in astonishment. "As a matter of fact, yes. You don't mean——?"

He nodded. "Exactly. Arrival at Chunga camp in late afternoon, with game-viewing on the river tomorrow morning, followed by Kafwala camp in the afternoon?"

"Yes, with pickup at two-thirty here by Homer?"

He shook his head. "Sorry about that. We're driving. Lisa's idea." He looked at her and added frankly, "Damn sorry about that, actually, but if I'll see you again the fates are smiling. You're——uh——what's the word they use these days, unattached?"

"A widow."

"Ought to say I'm sorry but can't. I like you."

She looked at him and began to laugh. "I really like your directness but I'm not accustomed, you know, to such——such——"

"Unabashed admiration? Can't think why not. You look alive," he said firmly. "Can't stand dull people."

"I'm very dull," Mrs. Pollifax told him sincerely. "I do volunteer work——not very efficiently——and raise geraniums and really——that is, in *general*," she added conscientiously, "live a very quiet life."

"Doesn't mean a thing," he said. "You look interested, a sense of wonder lingers. True?"

"I feel like a witness being cross-examined on the stand."

He nodded. "Bad habit of mine, the trouble with being a lawyer. My two children call it a deficiency——or rather, when they're pleased with me they say I'm direct, when they're angry I'm blunt."

"You have two children, then?"

He nodded. "Boy's thirty, the girl——that's Lisa——twenty-six. Raised them myself since their mother died, which happened when Lisa was three years old, and then said hands off, at least until two years ago. You've children?"

Mrs. Pollifax nodded. "Also a boy and a girl, both of them grown up and parents now. But what happened two years ago?"

"Had to rescue Lisa," he said, leaning back for the waiter to deposit dishes in front of them. "You can't imagine from what squalor," he added, "which wouldn't have mattered a tinker's damn if she was happy. Found her living in the East Village in New York doing social work, weight down to ninety-six pounds and crying her heart out over a chap she'd been in love with." He snorted indignantly. "Loved him, she said, because he cared. Trouble was the chap seems to have cared indiscriminately—about women mainly, I gather—and led her a merry chase. Considering Lisa graduated *magna cum laude* from Radcliffe it seemed very unintelligent of her."

"Emotions have nothing to do with intellect," pointed out Mrs. Pollifax.

"You understand that," he said, nodding. "Lisa didn't."

"What's happened to her since then?" asked Mrs. Pollifax.

"You'll see her," he reminded her. "Cool, brisk, businesslike, that's Lisa. Liked her better when she tumbled for every cause that came along. Warm-hearted, ardent child."

"Then of course she still is," put in Mrs. Pollifax.

"Somewhere, yes, but in the last two years she's grown a shell three feet thick. Thought the trip might do her good. Not healthy for either of us, living together. Exhausting."

Mrs. Pollifax put down her fork and smiled at him. "Is there anything that doesn't exhaust you?"

He directed a sleepy glance at her and smiled. "As a matter of fact a few things . . . good food, good talk, collecting rare books . . . still play a decent game of tennis and I've been known to rouse myself at dawn for bird-watching."

"That's hard to imagine. Are you," she asked sternly, "ecology-minded?"

"Passionately," he said with a straight face.

Mrs. Pollifax laughed and decided at that moment that if she had been deprived of Farrell's company during her few hours in Lusaka, then Cyrus Reed made a rather fair replacement. She also found herself hoping that Mr. Reed's lethargy was genuine, his daughter bona fide, and that he had not acquired a nasty habit of assassinating people in his spare time.

"Dessert?" suggested Mr. Reed, offering her the menu.

She glanced at her watch and shook her head. "I can only thank you for a delicious lunch," she told him, picking up her umbrella, "and see you next at Chunga."

They said goodbye and she removed herself to the lobby, where she chose a chair in sight of the front door. There she sat, gazing with interest at a party of dark men in turbans. A porter walked past her ringing a bicycle bell and carrying a chalkboard on which were scrawled the words "Mr. Kaacha wanted at desk," and then suddenly Homer Kulumbala appeared before her, smiling.

"Good afternoon, you are ready for Chunga?" he asked.

"Ready and waiting," she told him.

"Your luggage?"

She pointed to her suitcase next the door and he picked

it up and led her out to the hotel drive. The same VW
bus was parked among the bougainvillea, and again she
chose the front seat next to the driver. Homer went off
to round up other members of the safari and presently
returned escorting a narrow man in a pair of slacks and
a bush jacket. "Oh dear, we're twins," thought Mrs.
Pollifax ruefully, glancing from his bush jacket and slacks
to her own, and wondered if everyone on safari would
wear identical khaki clothes. "Hello," she said as he
reached the bus.

He was a prim-looking little man, perhaps forty-five or
fifty, his one notable feature a reddish-brown goatee. He
seemed an odd candidate for a safari: he looked fastidious
and a trifle pinched about the nostrils, as if the world
had a slightly rancid odor to him. At sight of Mrs. Pollifax he looked even more disapproving, or perhaps he
resented her occupying the front seat. He stepped carefully into the rear and in faintly accented English called
to Homer to be careful with his two suitcases. Only then
—and after wiping the seat with his handkerchief—did
he turn to Mrs. Pollifax and say peevishly, "They throw
them, have you noticed?"

"No," said Mrs. Pollifax, and introduced herself.

"Oh. Yes. Well." He extended a thin dry hand and
shook hers. "Kleiber here. Willem Kleiber." He did not
exactly wipe his hand after touching hers but she had
the impression that he wanted to, and that the gesture
was aborted only because he thought better of it.

"German?" she asked.

"No, no, Dutch," he said firmly.

If Mrs. Pollifax had feared that all bush outfits might
look alike, this idea was quickly dispelled now as Homer

escorted a third member of the safari to the bus. The woman walking beside him made Mrs. Pollifax feel suddenly dowdy and not at all swashbuckling. In her forties, she wore her long platinum hair tied in the back with a scarlet silk kerchief. Her bush jacket and slacks were cut out of pale-beige gabardine that very nearly matched the color of her hair, and they had been tailored to outline every curve of her figure. Diamonds glittered on several fingers, and a stunning turquoise was pinned to her black turtleneck shirt. Everything about her was striking, from her outfit to her cool sapphire eyes, the clear-cut features, pale-pink mouth and subtly tanned face.

". . . very nearly didn't stop, you know, and I was afraid I'd not be here in time, and then—oh, two already here, isn't this super," she said, stopping by the bus and smiling at Mr. Kleiber. "I think we'd better introduce ourselves, don't you?" Her voice was caressing, with a somewhat affected British accent, so that the word *better* emerged as *baytor*, spoken through the nose with a not unattractive nasal quality. "I'm Mrs. Lovecraft," she said. "*Amy* Lovecraft."

At this moment a tall, good-looking young man walked out of the hotel, shouted to Homer and then strode toward the bus calling, "I say, is this the transportation to Chunga camp for the KT/3 safari?"

"What a lovely man," murmured Mrs. Lovecraft appreciatively.

"Yes, yes," said Homer. "You are—?"

"John Steeves." He was dressed very casually in a heavy turtleneck sweater and shabby twill slacks; he looked, thought Mrs. Pollifax, like a man who would know that African mornings were cold. He looked sea-

soned. His voice marked him as an Englishman, the
patina on his boots marked him as a hiker. His face was
long and intense, with a thick brown mustache and
interesting dark eyes.

Homer's face lighted up at the name. "Of course—yes,
I was inquiring for you. Have you luggage?"

"A duffelbag, but Tom's bringing it. He's one of the
party, too, we met in the Coffee Hut. Tom Henry." He
turned and gestured vaguely toward the hotel entrance.
"There he is," he said.

Mrs. Pollifax turned and saw a solid-looking young
man walk out of the hotel carrying a suitcase and a
duffelbag, followed by a barefooted black boy carrying
a second suitcase. Tom Henry looked cheerful and un-
complicated, with sandy hair and a pair of level, candid
gray eyes. No nonsense about him, thought Mrs. Pollifax,
liking him at once; relaxed, stable and efficient. The boy
walking beside him suddenly looked up at him and
smiled. It was, thought Mrs. Pollifax, the most adoring
glance that she'd ever seen a child give an adult, and
she realized that the two belonged together.

"Henry?" said Homer, puzzled, and then, "Ah, this is
Doctor Henry? Dr. Henry from the mission hospital?"

"And Chanda," the young man said firmly. "Chanda
Henry."

The three men and the boy moved to the back of the
bus to stow away their luggage, and Mrs. Lovecraft
climbed in beside Mr. Kleiber, saying, "Isn't this fun?"

Glancing toward the hotel Mrs. Pollifax saw Cyrus
Reed walk out, looking vaguely concerned. He had exchanged his seersucker suit for a pair of new bluejeans
that made his legs look very long indeed, and over this

he wore a shirt and a shabby jacket. After noticing the bus he came toward it, and looking extraordinarily pleased at seeing her in it, he leaned over and spoke to her through the window.

"She's five hours late now," he said. "Difficulties mount."

At that moment a small red Fiat raced into the drive of the hotel and came to a sudden stop, its tires protesting shrilly. A voice called, "Dad!" and a young woman as petite as Reed was enormous jumped out of the car and waved. "I'm here, Judge!"

"That," said Cyrus Reed resignedly, "is Lisa."

"Judge?" asked Mrs. Pollifax.

"Retired."

She turned to look again at the young woman who was now opening the door of the car. She was slim and long-legged and difficult to overlook because her hair was bright auburn, the color of a new penny, and her face was round and pixie-like, with a dimple in the chin. Mrs. Pollifax said, "She doesn't look at all cold and business-like."

"She doesn't, does she," said Reed. He looked surprised. "Something's different. Like you to meet her. I'll bring her back."

Mrs. Pollifax watched as Lisa spoke to someone inside the car, and then from its confining interior crept a woman with a baby in a sling over her shoulders, followed by a small black man in a business suit and spectacles, three grinning barefooted boys, a bent old man carrying a crutch, and at last a young man in purple slacks and pink shirt. It was rather like that old circus act, thought Mrs. Pollifax, where dozens of people kept emerging from a tiny car, and she wondered how on earth they had all fitted inside. Lisa shook hands with each of them and then allowed herself to be led off to the minibus by her father.

". . . a flat tire," she was saying, "but Kanyama helped me change it and Mbulo was carrying firewood when I picked him up, so we had a jolly fire by the side of the road and cooked a breakfast. Really neat—and you should have seen the Falls!"

"I suppose you had to give rides to everyone?"

"Well, but wasn't it providential that I did? Otherwise I'd still be down near Penga somewhere with a flat tire. It's not at all like the States, Dad. Nobody asked for a ride, but how could I drive by them when I had a car and they didn't? Hello," she said, smiling warmly at Mrs. Pollifax. "Hello," she added, nodding to Mrs. Lovecraft and Mr. Kleiber.

"Well, you've not made it with much time to spare," said her father, sounding like fathers everywhere.

"Yes, but I made it, didn't I?" said Lisa, grinning. "And who's holding us up now? See you all later," she called over her shoulder, and began propelling her father toward the hotel.

On the way to the entrance they passed Homer carrying luggage for another guest. The Reeds stopped to speak to him, leaving the newest member of the party waiting patiently, a faint smile on his lips. He was a man of average height, perhaps fifty, carrying an attaché case and a battered trench coat over his arm. He was still dressed for traveling, Mrs. Pollifax noted, in a light suit that must once have been well-cut but was wrinkled now.

He wore his hair rather long; it was jet black, with streaks of pure white.

The group abruptly dissolved and Homer came toward them smiling. "We now have Mr. McIntosh," he said, gesturing at the man beside him. "We go. Gentlemen, if you will be so kind as to get in the bus now?"

The two men and the boy Chanda climbed into the seat in the far rear, next the luggage. Mr. McIntosh crawled past Mrs. Lovecraft to sit in the space between her and Mr. Kleiber. Homer closed and locked the doors and a moment later they were off, driving on the left side of the road like the British.

They passed the National Assembly building with its roof sheathed in copper and gleaming in the sun. They passed neat rows of government housing and then a shantytown with thatched-roof huts, and finally, leaving the city behind, a satellite station that had been built by the Japanese, Homer told them. As the traffic thinned they sped past fields of cotton, sunflowers and maize, and the pedestrians along the side of the road increased: women walking with loads of firewood balanced carefully on their heads, a few men wheeling bicycles. Then these, too, vanished and they settled down to the long road ahead, moving steadily toward the Mungwa mountain range. The sun began to look surprisingly low on the horizon to Mrs. Pollifax, and when she commented on this she was startled to learn that in Zambia the sun set at six o'clock. She began to understand some of the urgency behind Homer's driving; certainly he drove like a man pursued by *something*, and now it was heartening to realize the something was darkness, because she had no desire to be caught among wild animals in the dark either. The excessive speed rendered conversation almost impossible, however; everything rattled and it was necessary to cling to one's seat.

An hour later Mrs. Pollifax was still clinging to her seat when Homer placed his foot on the brake and nearly sent her through the windshield. Up ahead she saw a roadblock, a gaily striped red-and-white pole extending from one side of the road to the other.

From the rear Mr. Kleiber called, "And what is this?"

"The bridge," said Homer. "All our bridges are guarded by the police."

"Good heavens why?" asked Mrs. Pollifax, turning to look at him in surprise.

"Rhodesian spies," he said with a shrug. "They try to bomb our bridges. We have three in Zambia, all of them over the Kafue River." He pronounced it *Ka-fooey*.

"Rhodesian *spies*?" repeated Mrs. Pollifax.

"Yes, spies. They are everywhere." With a jerk of his head to the left he added, "The police live over there."

Mrs. Pollifax glancd to the left and saw a cluster of corrugated tin houses down near the river, shaded by a circle of acacia trees. She started to speak but Homer's attention had turned to the guard who walked toward them, looking very official with a rifle strapped across his back. He wore a felt cavalry hat, blue khaki shorts and tunic, and around his legs a wrapping of heavy cloth from ankle to knee that could only be puttees, decided Mrs. Pollifax, remembering Kipling. He peered into the car and then shook hands with Homer and began talking in an incomprehensible language that Homer seemed to understand. At last the guard saluted, the bus was put into gear and they moved across the modest bridge over the river. "What language was it that you spoke back there?" asked Mrs. Pollifax.

"Nyanga," said Homer. "I speak Tonga, he speaks Luvale but we both know Nyanga. All the government people know Nyanga."

"Those spies you mentioned," began Mrs. Pollifax, and then found it even more difficult to be heard as they turned off the paved highway onto a dirt road marked by a sign that read CHUNGA CAMP. "Those spies," she shouted above the rattles and bumps, hanging onto her seat with both hands to keep from hitting the roof of the bus.

"What?" shouted Homer.

"Spies," she shrieked. Just as she decided that the road had been cut out of a pitted lava bed it changed to brown dust beaten hard into corrugated stripes that placed her more firmly in her seat but vibrated her spine like a massage.

Homer neatly steered the bus around a hole and shouted back, "They spy on freedom fighters. In the Southern Province they used to cross the border from Rhodesia and kidnap people, set land mines and kill. There is not so much there now, but still they sneak in. A month ago they set a bomb in Lusaka, at private home, and killed Mr. Chitepo, Rhodesian black nationalist in the African National Congress."

"Who did?" shouted Mrs. Polifax. "Who would do such a thing?"

Homer shrugged. "Mercenaries. Rhodesian police agents. Spies."

Mrs. Pollifax rested her voice while she attached this diverting piece of news to certain facts casually men-

tioned in the pamphlets that Bishop had deposited with
her last week. She remembered that until recently Zambia
had been a lonely bastion of black independence in the
center of Africa, bounded on the east by Portuguese-ruled
Mozambique, on the west by Portuguese-ruled Angola,
with Rhodesia flanking its southern border, backed up by
South Africa below it. That had been Zambia's situation
when it finally threw off the last shackles of white rule
in 1964.

At the time of its independence, however, Zambia had
found itself still bound to Rhodesia by roads, electric
power, rail routes and economic ties. A man who loathed
apartheid and who dedicated himself to working against
it, President Kaunda had set out at once to loosen those
ties, enlisting the help of the Chinese to build a railway
to the north, and the Italians to build a new dam. The
price of rejecting any dependence on Rhodesia had been
severe: during one crisis the country had been forced to
export its copper by trucks over a road that came to be
called the "Hell Run." Zambia had survived, however,
and she supposed that it was proof of President Kaunda's
genius that it had not only survived economically but had
remained involved in and supportive of the liberation
movements in her neighboring countries. Those were the
words the pamphlet had used: *involved* and *supportive*.
Embroiled sounded more appropriate, she thought dryly;
certainly nothing had been said about spies, land mines
and kidnapings.

Now of course, both Mozambique and Angola had won
their independence after years of guerilla warfare and
bloodshed, and Rhodesia and South Africa stood alone
as rigid defenders of white supremacy. But she had for-

gotten—it came back to her now—that sometime during the worst of the infighting Rhodesia had angrily closed her borders to Zambia, precipitating even more strains on the Zambian economy. A pity, she thought, that taking a stand on moral issues had to prove so lonely these days, but apparently the closure was only a formal one if spies streamed back and forth. She remembered that the phrase "freedom fighters" had been mentioned, too, in one of those pocket histories.

"Freedom fighters," she shouted at Homer's profile. "Who are they?"

"Liberation leaders," he called back at her. "Refugees. They escape to Zambia with a price on their heads, or prison sentences. They stay, they train, they go back. Quietly, you understand?"

"Yes," said Mrs. Pollifax, nodding. "I just didn't realize it was still—uh—continuing."

He nodded vigorously. "But the leaders begin to talk now. South Africa grows very worried, she fears a race war in Africa and pushes Rhodesia to talk, loosen up. We have a saying: '*Ukupangile nsofu kano uli ne fumo.* Before you can talk of killing an elephant you must first be equipped with a spear.'" He grinned and slowed the minibus. "And speaking of elephants, there is your first elephant, everyone. You wish pictures?"

Exclamations rose from the rear, but Mrs. Pollifax could only gasp and stare. Her first elephant stood scarcely fifteen feet away, grazing contentedly on the leaves at the top of a tree, his huge gray frame bleached by dust, his flaplike ears cocked as if he knew very well they were there. Slowly he turned his ponderous head and looked at the minibus with beady interested eyes. Mrs. Pollifax was certain that he stared directly at her. She gave him a delighted, grateful smile before she lifted her camera and snapped his picture.

They drove on, reaching another road barrier, this one manned by an amiable young park guard. After slowing down to allow a family of baboons to cross the road, Mrs. Pollifax glimpsed the thatched tops of buildings ahead. They entered a clearing, passed a gas pump, a cluster of rondevaals with thatched roofs, and coasted to a stop near a sloping riverbank.

"Is this Chunga camp?" called Mrs. Lovecraft.

Homer shook his head. "This is noncatering section, for weekend campers only. We wait now for the boat. There should be a boat," he said, frowning, and climbed out and stared across the river at what looked to be an island.

Mrs. Pollifax opened the door beside her and jumped down to stretch her legs. The others stirred too, and climbed out, smiling at each other a little uncertainly. Mrs. Lovecraft strolled over to join Homer, and after a moment Mr. McIntosh and Mr. Kleiber followed her. The sun had disappeared behind a cloud, draining all color from the landscape, and Mrs. Pollifax felt suddenly very small under the huge silvery sky as she waited for a mysterious boat that showed no signs of appearing on that vast flat expanse of silky gray water.

"There," said Homer suddenly, pointing. "The boat."

A small speck had appeared on the gray water, looking almost spectral as it rounded the point. It veered, grew larger, became an object totally unlike a boat, and then as it moved toward them, one man at the stern, she began to hear the sound of its motor and she realized it was a pontoon boat, nearly flat and propelled by an outboard motor.

"Good, let's help with all this luggage," Dr. Henry said, and walked around to the back of the bus and began handing suitcases to Chanda. There was a whispered discussion between them and then he said, "No, no, you give it to her." Holding up Mrs. Pollifax's gay umbrella he said, "Chanda tells me this is yours?"

"Yes, but how on earth did he know?" she asked in surprise.

Dr. Henry laughed. "I couldn't possibly tell you, but he always knows these things. He says he looked inside of you and saw colors to match. *Mukolamfula* was the word which, if the little Bemba I've learned is right, means rainbow."

"I'm very touched," she said, smiling at Chanda.

The boy handed her the umbrella, grinned, ducked his head shyly and went back for another suitcase. Behind her the boat had just landed, the slant of its bow dovetailing perfectly with the slant of the riverbank. Homer said, "The boat will come back for the luggage, it is very safe here. You will get in now, please?"

They distributed themselves on packing cases; the boat was pushed away from the shore, the motor sputtered, they turned and began the trip toward the distant shore, any conversation rendered frivolous by the awesome silence of the river. The only sounds were of the water streaming past the bow, leaving a frothy wake behind them, and the murmur of Homer's voice as he spoke quietly to the boy at the wheel. The air was cool, full of fragrances, and as they chugged their way toward the opposite bank the smell of a wood fire became distinct.

Suddenly the sun reappeared, very low on the horizon now, and as the boat rounded the point Mrs. Pollifax had her first view of Chunga camp. She saw another sloping riverbank cut out of the trees, with a narrow wharf jutting into the water. Smoke from a campfire drifted lazily across the clearing, threading its way through the palms. Off to the left there was a long white building with a thatched roof, and behind this, spaced at intervals up and down a gently sloping hill, stood narrow cabins built of reed and thatch.

The sound of the boat had brought a handful of people down to the landing, all of their faces black. One in particular stood out from the others, a broad-shouldered young man in forest-green tunic and shorts. His smile as the boat reached the weathered gray dock was as broad as his shoulders, a brilliant slash of white that met and warmed two laughing eyes.

"Welcome to Chunga," he said as the boat slid up to the wharf. "I'm Julian, your safari manager. If you will come in and register—?"

Mrs. Pollifax was the first to enter the small office near the landing. Julian handed her registration forms and a pen and she brought out her passport and copied down its numbers. Over her shoulder Julian called instructions to the boy who had brought them in the boat, and a moment later she heard the sound of the motor on the water. "Besides the luggage," he explained to her, "there are two more guests coming soon from Lusaka."

"Yes, I know," she said, "I met them."

His huge white smile blossomed again. "Then you have already two friends, good. Moses takes you up now, you'll be in Leopard cabin."

Moses wore dusty sneakers and bright-blue slacks. She turned and followed him up a gravel path. The reborn sun was meeting the horizon now, its light no longer clear gold but a hot amber that rusted the soil a deeper red. Along the path leaves crackled underfoot like dry parchment, and Mrs. Pollifax shivered in the sudden coolness. When they reached the cabin marked Leopard, Moses carried her suitcase up four wooden stairs and placed it beside the door, and then he stood and explained that there was a shower and pointed vaguely off into the distance. Mrs. Pollifax, her mind now on sweaters, blankets and hot coffee, shook her head, thanked him and scurried up the steps into the cabin. As she turned to close the wooden door behind her the sun slipped over the horizon with finality. Homer had been absolutely correct: it was just six o'clock.

CHAPTER

5

It was dim inside the cabin. Two small screened windows were heavily shaded by the thatch roof but an electric-light bulb dangled over the night table and Mrs. Pollifax snapped it on. The pair of narrow beds looked oddly bridelike: they were sealed inside of white mosquito netting that flowed like bridal veils from the ceiling and were tucked firmly under each mattress, rendering each bed nearly inaccessible. Frustrated, she deposited her suitcase on the floor until she saw a luggage rack behind the door and placed it there instead, and then, looking around her she said aloud, "Well—I'm *here*."

And so, presumably, was Aristotle, she reminded herself.

It was incredibly, starkly quiet . . . Something fell to the ground outside her cabin; it sounded like fruit dropping from a tree. A faint breeze rustled the reed walls and then subsided, and she could hear the distant hum of a generator. Presently voices inserted themselves into this bottomless quiet; she heard a girl laugh, a man reply and recognized Cyrus Reed's voice: so he and Lisa had arrived. She opened her suitcase and quickly changed into a heavy sweater, combed her hair, checked the film in her camera and picked up her jacket. When she opened the door a lizard slid across the step and vanished under the cabin. Carrying her flashlight she walked down the path toward the water, hesitated, and then passed through an empty, brightly lighted bar into the dining hall. Just beyond its low wall a campfire was burning in the cleared area overlooking the river. A dozen chairs encircled it, and one of them was occupied by John Steeves.

Seeing her he rose and gave her a quick, rather shy smile that lighted up his serious face. "I don't believe I know your name," he said, holding out a hand. "I'm John Steeves."

"Emily Pollifax," she told him, shaking hands with him. "Do sit down. I love this fire. I'm going to sit as close as I dare because actually I'm freezing."

"I know," he said, nodding. "It's really early spring here, and a rather late rainy season too, they tell me, which is why the roads haven't been graded yet. As perhaps you noticed," he said with a grin.

She realized that he was much older than she'd thought at first. Everything about him was boyish—his relatively unlined face, his slouch, his vitality—except for his eyes: there was something haunted about his eyes, as if they'd seen too much. They were what her son Roger would call the eyes of an old soul, so that she now added quite a few years to her original impression and guessed him to be in his middle thirties.

"Looking forward to the safari?" he asked, and Mrs. Pollifax realized that she'd been staring at him.

"Oh yes indeed," she told him warmly. "And you?"

He nodded. "Bit of a rest for me. Too much traveling spoils one for resorts and the really plush places."

"You travel a great deal, then?"

He nodded, extended one lean leg and poked at the fire with his shabby boot. "Write travel books," he said.

"Steeves," she mused. "I'm afraid—"

"I know," he said with that sudden blaze of a smile that so transformed him. "People never remember authors' names."

"Tell me the titles of your books, then."

"Mmmmm . . . *Lost in the Himalayas, At Home in the Andes*, followed by *Over the Chinese Border* and *One Hundred Nights in a Mongolian Yurt*."

"But of course," she exclaimed. "I read *Over the Chinese Border* and enjoyed it tremendously. You disguise yourself and live among the natives."

He grinned. "You might say disguise is the main ingredient of my success, yes. A bit of the actor in me, you know, I love fooling around with makeup. Actually I began as an actor, but it's much more fun applying it all to dangerous situations."

"You like danger?" she asked curiously.

"It certainly beats the humdrum routine of ordinary living," he said ruefully.

"Yes," agreed Mrs. Pollifax, smiling faintly. "The exhilaration. The things one learns about oneself. The total immersion in the moment."

He looked at her in surprise, as if he'd not expected this from her. "You seem to have experienced something of it—" His glance moved beyond Mrs. Pollifax and he stopped speaking, a curious expression on his face. She turned and saw Lisa Reed walking toward them, her father just emerging from the dining hall behind her.

Steeves rose to his feet, looking impressed. "I say—good evening. You weren't on the bus with us, are you in the safari group too?"

Lisa had changed into bluejeans and a denim shirt and in them she looked younger, more vulnerable, her fashionable leanness replaced by a fragile quality. It occurred to Mrs. Pollifax that she was blushing; certainly her gamine face had turned a darker color but her voice when she spoke was impersonal. "Yes, we came by car from Lusaka. I'm Lisa Reed."

"And Cyrus Reed, parent," added her father. Sinking into the chair beside Mrs. Pollifax he smiled at her and said, "Good to see you again."

Steeves looked pleased. "Americans, are you? I do wish you'd sit down over here—I've not met an American in years. Perhaps you can explain to me what's been happening in your country."

"Lisa can if anyone can," said Reed. "A biased account, naturally."

Steeves flashed his quick, radiant smile. "But all accounts are biased, surely? You had something called a watershed affair?"

That won a smile from Lisa. "No, no," she said, sitting down next to him, and began speaking with quick gestures, her face very serious, her slender hands cutting the air with incisive slashes.

Her father turned to Mrs. Pollifax. "Thought you'd like to know, by the way, that someone was asking for you at the hotel when I checked out."

"Asking for me?" gasped Mrs. Pollifax. "Was he tall, with dark hair and blue eyes and—"

Reed shook his head. "Zambian. Short black chap. Dressed in a kind of—well," he said, looking pained, "it had hibiscus all over it. Or bougainvillea. That sort of shirt, with black trousers and sneakers."

Puzzled, Mrs. Pollifax said, "And you're quite sure he was asking for *me*?"

"Clearly," nodded Reed. "Couldn't help but overhear. Asked for your room number, the clerk said you'd already checked out, he left."

"How very odd," said Mrs. Pollifax, frowning. "There's that advertisement, of course, but it won't be published in the *Times of Zambia* until tomorrow morning."

Her companion nodded. "Unless the typesetter knows someone who knows someone who knows your friend. Or perhaps the travel bureau sent a chap along to make sure you'd gotten off on time." With a gesture toward the other two he said, "Damn glad to see there's someone young and male for Lisa."

Mrs. Pollifax wrenched her thoughts away from the mysterious man at the hotel. "I thought," she said, "that your daughter blushed when she saw him."

His brows lifted. "Thought so, did you?" He turned and gazed at Lisa with interest. "Amazing. I missed that."

"You were standing behind her."

"So I was. Seems an engaging fellow, Steeves."

John Steeves was certainly being very attentive, thought

Mrs. Pollifax, glancing at the two across the campfire: those haunted eyes of his were fixed intently on Lisa's face as he listened, his quick smile occasionally transforming their sadness. It was a rare person who listened like that, reflected Mrs. Pollifax, and thought it a quality difficult for any woman to resist.

"And you?" asked Reed, directing his quizzical glance at her. "Always travel alone?"

"Oh yes," she said simply. "At least—"

"At least you start off alone," he said with his slow smile, "and then collect people like a Pied Piper? Ah, here comes whatsisname. Dour fellow you rode out with."

"Mr. Kleiber," she reminded him. "Willem Kleiber."

Mr. Kleiber approached the fire hesitantly, sat down two chairs removed from Cyrus Reed and said distastefully, "There is a *complete* absence of running water here. Exactly how does one wash?"

"The word *safari*," said Reed in an offhand voice, "means camping, you know."

Lisa had turned at the sound of his voice. "There are shower pipes behind those reed fences, you know. Hot water too."

Mr. Kleiber's nose looked, if anything, even more pinched; he had the most active nostrils of anyone she'd met, thought Mrs. Pollifax. "Anyone can walk in," he said coldly. "Anyone. There's no door, there's no roof."

In a rather amused voice Steeves said, "I really don't think anyone would want to, you know. Try singing loudly while you're under the tap."

"That's just what *I* did," said Amy Lovecraft, strolling into the circle and joining them. She was looking very elegant in snug black pants, a cashmere sweater and a

short suede jacket. She chose the seat on the other side
of John Steeves and sat down, placed a hand on his arm
and smiled into his face. "I do hope we're on a first-
name basis now so that I can call you John."

"Please do," he said politely. "Have you met Lisa
Reed?"

"No, duck," she said and, leaning forward, gave Lisa
a much less enthusiastic smile. "I've not met that lovely
huge man over there, either."

"We're both Reeds," Lisa said shortly. "I'm Lisa and
he's my father Cyrus, and that's Mrs. Pollifax next him."

"Delighted, Cyrus," said Mrs. Lovecraft, giving him a
warm smile and ignoring Mrs. Pollifax. "And here comes
Tom Henry. I think it's super our having a doctor with
us as well as a noted travel writer, don't you?"

This was tactless, thought Mrs. Pollifax, and quite
enough to antagonize the remaining men, but if she
decided to reserve judgment on Mrs. Lovecraft for the
moment she could welcome Dr. Henry wholeheartedly.
He sat down next to her, crossed his legs, gave her a
cheerful smile and said, "I hope dinner's soon, I'm starving."

"About five more minutes," Mrs. Pollifax told him
after a glance at her watch. "Or just enough time to ask
what Homer meant when he said you're at a mission
hospital. Does that mean you live here in Zambia?"

He wrenched his eyes from Lisa Reed and turned to
give her his full attention. "Yes it does—the hospital's
over on the Zambesi River near the Angolan border. I
came out from Canada three years ago and I'm sure all
my friends expected me back in Windsor a week later."

He gave her a sidelong boyish smile. "Needless to say I'm still here."

"You like it."

"Love it," he admitted. "So much so that I wanted to try a safari on my seven days' leave. There's so much about the bush I've been too busy to learn, and a great deal about wild animals I want to learn."

"Including *Homo sapiens*?" said Cyrus Reed, leaning forward to enter the conversation.

"Well, I see a good many of *them*," said Dr. Henry, smiling back, "but aside from several missionary families at the hospital it's been a long time since I've seen a group like this. I'd forgotten," he said dryly, "what a lot of nonsense people talk."

Cyrus Reed smiled. "I agree with you completely."

"What do you talk about at your hospital when you're relaxing?" asked Mrs. Pollifax.

He grinned. "Oh—life, death, septicemia, who's due to boil the next drinking water, or what the village witch doctor said that day."

Mrs. Pollifax laughed. "Scarcely small talk."

"God, no." He looked chagrined. "Obviously I'll have to brush up on that." He smiled at Chanda as the boy walked into the campfire circle and came to stand beside him. "*Bweleniko*," he said. "*Mwapoleni*."

"*Kuntu kuli kusuma*," the boy said, smiling.

"*Endita*." Turning to Mrs. Pollifax he said, "Chanda talks Bemba but he speaks a little English now and understands it very well. When we first met I was struggling to learn Nyanga, and now I'm having to learn Bemba, and it all grows rather confusing. Chanda, you've not met this gentleman yet. He's Mr. Cyrus Reed."

Chanda stepped forward and shook hands with Reed and then, to their surprise, clapped his hands three times. "That's the Zambian greeting," explained Dr. Henry with a grin. "Chanda's given you only the modified version. When it's done properly it's repeated three times . . . a handshake followed by three claps and then another round or two. Quite a ceremony."

"Certainly feel thoroughly greeted," admitted Reed.

Somewhat removed from them, Willem Kleiber said in alarm, "He's not—uh—yours, is he?"

Tom Henry's smile was friendly. "He is now. He was brought into the hospital half-dead, his entire village wiped out by fighting on the Angolan border. Freedom fighters brought him in."

Overhearing this, Lisa gasped, "You live there?"

He nodded.

"But that must be fascinating."

"It is," he said, meeting her glance with a faint smile.

At that moment a drum began beating to announce dinner. Mrs. Pollifax turned and saw that in the open-air dining room behind her a huge tureen was being carried in by a boy in a white jacket. She also saw Mr. McIntosh standing on the step, hesitating between them and the dining hall. He had changed into khaki slacks over which he wore a white shirt open at the neck and a black V-neck sweater, and she wondered if he was going to appear late at every meal and leave early, like a shadow. Intuitively she felt that he was an intensely private, introverted man, but having decided this she wondered how: was it the manner in which he looked out from under his brows, head slightly bent? or was it that his smile, which was surprisingly sweet, never changed or wavered? He simply stood and waited, smiling, while they left their chairs and moved toward him, and then, still smiling, he turned and walked toward the buffet table and placed himself in line.

With the arrival of McIntosh Mrs. Pollifax realized the safari group was now complete and she wondered, not for the first time, which of these people could be an assassin. Now that she'd met them all she found this a very jarring thought because they all looked so normal, even wholesome, and certainly all of them were—well, explainable, she reasoned, reaching for a word that eliminated the existence of sinister motives and façades. She could not imagine any of them a professional killer standing in a crowd with a gun in his pocket, waiting, measuring, judging, whipping out the gun and firing, then vanishing into the crowd. In the first place, none of these people looked capable of such brutal violence, and in the second place she couldn't imagine any of them managing such a thing without being noticed.

Cyrus Reed would certainly be noticed, she thought with an amused glance at him towering over the soup tureen. It was possible that without his goatee Mr. Kleiber might look sufficiently nondescript; it was also possible that Tom Henry was not a doctor at all. McIntosh, she thought, would certainly melt into a crowd—he was doing so right now; John Steeves was too distinguished to melt, but she knew from his books that he was a genius at disguising himself.

If Carstairs was right, she thought, one of them had to be wearing a devilishly clever mask . . . and then she recalled with interest Carstairs' telephone call to her the evening before she left New Jersey. She had assured him that yes, her passport had been returned safely to her and that yes, Bishop had explained the importance of the snapshots, and then she had asked him the question that had begun to exasperate her. "I realize this is an insane world," she, had told him, "but can you please tell me why an assassin would go on a *safari*?"

"Why, to meet someone, I imagine," Carstairs had said pleasantly. "Plan the next assassination, perhaps, or be paid for the last one. Certainly not for *fun*."

If this was true—and Carstairs' suppositions nearly always proved sound—there could be two people wearing masks on this safari, each watching the others and wondering, as she was doing . . . and this meant that eventually they would have to go off together for a good little chat, didn't it? It occurred to her that if she was very observant and very discreet she might be able to do a little eavesdropping . . .

Of course Carstairs had made it very clear to her that she was to do nothing but take photographs, and she planned to do a very *good* job with her picture-taking, but now that she thought about it, it seemed incredible waste for her to be here on the spot and not do a little spying as well. After all, it was taxpayers' money that was paying for her safari, she thought virtuously, and as a taxpayer herself she abhorred waste.

Besides, she added, dropping all pretense at justification, it would be such fun to surprise Carstairs and catch Aristotle.

CHAPTER

6

In the morning the safari officially began with the game-viewing excursion up the river before leaving for Kafwala camp. Mrs. Pollifax came to breakfast early and still a little sleepy, for it was barely seven and she'd not slept with any continuity. The walls of her cabin had rustled all night—she was convinced that some small animal lived in them—and at one point she had awakened to a loud animal cry, followed by a soft whistle and the pounding of feet. After this another fruit had dropped from the tree outside her cabin, and the reeds had begun to whisper again . . . At breakfast Julian told her that animals roamed freely through the camp at night, that a hippo had been heard and that pukus, who liked the safety of the camp at night, made soft whistling sounds. It was just as well she'd not known, she reflected, or she might never have dared fall asleep again.

"I want you to meet Crispin now," Julian said as they rose from the breakfast table. "I will be staying at camp to make final arrangements for our trip at noon, and Crispin will take you game-viewing. He's assistant safari manager and he'll be with us for the entire safari."

Crispin was not in uniform, and looked surprisingly like an eager schoolboy in his flowered shirt, dark trousers and sneakers. He had a long slender face and bright, interested eyes. He actually looked excited about taking them out game-viewing, and Mrs. Pollifax found this rather endearing.

John Steeves said, "Crispin's even more English than Julian. What are your Zambian names?"

"Mine?" Julian laughed. "You want it all at once? Milimo Simoko Chikwanda."

Steeves grinned. "I'll call you Julian. And Crispin's?"

"Wamufu Chinyanta Muchona."

Steeves nodded. "Definitely Julian and Crispin."

"I think so," Julian said in amusement.

There was a charming picnic air about the excursion up the river. The sun was soft and golden, the river full of morning sounds, and they traveled on a splendid breakfast of bacon and eggs, sausage, toast and coffee. Mr. Kleiber, sitting next to Mrs. Pollifax, went so far as to confide that he would like to see a crocodile. Across the aisle Amy Lovecraft had blossomed out with a professional-looking camera loaded with all kinds of attachments that she tried to explain to John Steeves. The Reeds sat together in front, both looking sleepy; Tom Henry and Chanda stood in the stern of the boat and

McIntosh by himself in the bow; he too bristled with cameras and light meters.

Abruptly Crispin called out to the boy at the wheel, gestured, and the launch headed across to the opposite bank, at which point Mrs. Pollifax lifted her camera and took a picture of the river ahead, managing to capture several profiles at the same time. She had already taken a snapshot of everyone climbing into the boat and no one seemed to have minded except Cyrus Reed, who had glanced at her reproachfully, as if he'd not expected this of her.

"Hippo," said Crispin in a low voice, and pointed.

Every head turned to the left, the launch slowed and they coasted toward a cleft in the tangle of roots and trees that lined the riverbank. Slowly they drew abreast of a dark, secret-looking inlet of water that flowed into the river, and as they reached this narrow tributary Mrs. Pollifax looked deep into its shadows and saw enormous shapes moving through the trees, and suddenly heard a thunderous roar as the first hippo plunged into the stream. Patches of sunlight glinted across monstrous black heads as the hippos floated and bobbed out into the river. She counted five, six, seven hippos and gave up counting at eleven. They kept coming, whole families snorting and cavorting with ponderous mischievousness, one of the bolder ones swimming out near the launch to give them all a curious stare.

Mrs. Pollifax laughed, and when the launch resumed its trip upriver the others were smiling too and began to talk and move about the boat. McIntosh peeled off his jacket and came to stand next to Mrs. Pollifax, his camera at the ready. Without his jacket, only a short-sleeved polo shirt remained and she thought it made him look rather flat-chested. His posture was not good but then, she thought forgivingly, it would be impossible for anyone to stand erect if they insisted on peering out at the world from under their eyebrows; a certain amount of slumping was compulsive. She noticed that his longish black hair badly needed a shampoo but the threads of white in it were dramatic against his tanned face.

"I hope you don't mind," he said with his faint smile, and sat down on the edge of the bench next her, his eyes on the shoreline.

"Not at all," she said. "That's a handsome camera you have. I've been admiring it."

He glanced at her, his smile deepening, and told her what kind it was.

"Lovely," she said, not understanding a word, and then with a bright smile, "Where do you make your home, Mr. McIntosh?"

"Pretty much out of my attaché case," he said, smiling.

"But you're American, aren't you?"

"An American citizen, yes."

"Then do you," she asked reasonably, "live in the United States?"

"Not really," he said, smiling. "I come and go." He lifted his camera and snapped a picture of the riverbank, and then as Crispin called out "Egret!" he slipped away from her to the rear of the boat.

Behind her Amy Lovecraft leaned forward and said, "He's impossible to talk to, isn't he? I couldn't even get a direct yes or no from him on whether he's married. I mean, surely that's something you could answer yes or no to? A man either has a wife or he hasn't."

Mrs. Pollifax turned to smile into her vivid sapphire-blue eyes. "You have a point there, although of course these days such matters are sometimes—"

"What's more," said Mrs. Lovecraft, lowering her voice, "I don't think McIntosh is his last name at all."

At this Mrs. Pollifax turned completely to face her. "Good heavens," she murmured, "really?"

Mrs. Lovecraft nodded. "When we registered at Chunga," she said, her voice becoming conspiratorial, "I was standing next him and I caught a glimpse of his passport. McIntosh is his *first* name. There was an entirely different name following it, something that began with an M too, but I couldn't make it out. And," she added indignantly, "I've never seen an American passport with the last name first. Julian may have accepted him as Mr. McIntosh because he doesn't *know*, but take a look at your own passport sometime: the last name *doesn't* come first."

"Amy," called Steeves from across the aisle, "you wanted to see some impala, take a look over here."

Mrs. Lovecraft jumped up, leaving Mrs. Pollifax to digest this interesting piece of information. *Not* a sensible woman, thought Mrs. Pollifax, watching her leave; stupid of her to go about saying such things, indebted as Mrs. Pollifax was to her for the news. She might have thought it exposed McIntosh, but it also betrayed her spitefulness at being ignored by him. She wondered if Amy Lovecraft's life had been difficult: she was a very attractive woman and must once have been lovely, but so very often beautiful women grew up lopsided or didn't grow at all. She thought there was a curious hardness about her, as if her beauty was a deceptively rich topsoil, thinly spread over rock. . . . Finding that no one was looking in her direction, Mrs. Pollifax reached into her purse and surreptitiously examined her passport. Mrs. Lovecraft was absolutely right: there was no juxtaposition of names, the given name came first.

"Having fun?" asked Cyrus Reed, walking up the aisle.

"Oh yes," she said, beaming at him, and then, thinking of what Mrs. Lovecraft had just told her, she added, "and I'm learning so much, it's really so educational."

At midmorning they stopped briefly at an abandoned ferry crossing where the remains of a road cut like a knife through the tall grass. Crispin allowed them to climb out for a moment and walk a few cautious paces down the road. "But not far," he said firmly. "Not without a guard."

"Why should we need a guard?" protested Mrs. Pollifax.

"It's dangerous."

She looked out upon the peaceful scene, at bright petunia-like flowers blooming by the roadside, at a landscape empty of all movement, and she was incredulous. "But it looks so safe!"

Tom Henry grinned. "It does, doesn't it? But we're near the river, you know, which means if you left the road you might stumble across a crocodile sunning itself in the mud. Failing that, there are puff adders, pythons, black mambas and bushwangers, not to mention the possibility of a rhino or hippo who might be in an ugly temper."

"Oh," said Mrs. Pollifax, taken aback.

Crispin said, "You treat many snake bites at your hospital, Doctor?"

"Maybe not so successfully as your village medicine men," said Tom, "but we save a few. Speaking of medicine men, it's certainly humbling to realize that people here evolved their own vaccine centuries before we did in the laboratories."

Crispin said modestly, "We are in the position to learn, you know. We see the mongoose fight with a poisonous snake, he is bitten, he runs to a certain bush and eats the leaves and lives. The medicine man studies all these signs."

Steeves said, "And which do you visit, Crispin, when you feel ill?"

Crispin grinned. "I would go first to the medical doctor," he said, his eyes laughing, "and then I would visit the medicine man just to be sure."

"Covering all your bets," chuckled Dr. Henry as they climbed back into the boat.

Lisa, standing on the bank next to Mrs. Pollifax, said in a low voice, "Care to bet whose arms Mrs. Lovecraft is going to fall into?"

She had misjudged her, however; Amy Lovecraft graciously accepted Crispin's hand, stepped onto the bow of the boat and remained there for a long moment, her profile turned to the sky, before allowing John Steeves to help her inside.

"What's your deadliest snake?" Reed asked Crispin, which brought a laugh from Lisa.

"Oh the viper," he said. "You are bitten, and in ten minutes you die."

"Good heavens!"

"The black mamba is second, killing in ten or fifteen minutes. If you go to the zoo in Lusaka the snake man will tell you all about it. He will also tell you snakes neither see nor hear, they only sense vibrations." He grinned. "Therefore if you meet a snake and stand perfectly still it won't find you."

"I couldn't possibly stand still," said Lisa, shivering. "I'd run like blazes."

Mrs. Pollifax looked at Crispin, and then she looked at the dark, jungle-like banks of the river lined with twisted roots like claws, deep shadows, tangles of brush and palm and the white tracery of dead roots. She thought of the disciplines needed in this country to avoid sudden painful death and she acknowledged ruefully that survival here was a trifle different from crossing on the green light.

Some forty-five minutes later they reached Chunga camp again. They had seen an egret, a cormorant and a group of impala and hippos, and Julian was waiting on the dock to tell Mrs. Pollifax that a policeman from Lusaka had arrived to ask her questions.

"He arrived fifteen minutes ago," Julian said, helping her out of the launch, "and I told him I will bring you to him. He's seated over there in a chair behind the trees, very private."

There was no curiosity in Julian's candid gaze; in Mrs. Pollifax, however, there was considerable curiosity and she admitted to being startled. "You're quite certain it's me he wants to see?"

"Oh yes," said Julian simply, "he has driven all the way from Lusaka to see you."

"That's a long drive."

"Anything wrong?" asked Cyrus Reed.

Mrs. Pollifax realized that she had been the first person off the boat and now the others had arrived behind her and were listening. She smiled, shook her head and followed Julian to the appointed place, which was indeed private, being nearly encircled by palms. A slender young man in a dark-blue uniform rose. He looked self-contained and very polite, his black face thin and intelligent. "Mrs. Pollifax?"

She assured him that she was Mrs. Pollifax and sat down.

A small table had been placed in front of him on which rested a half-finished Coke and a notebook. He now placed the notebook on his lap and drew out a pen.

"I have come, madam," he said, pronouncing the word m'domm, "to inquire about your advertisement in this morning's *Times of Zambia*. A most curious advertisement, surely?"

"My adver—oh," she said, comprehension dawning, "it's been published today? I'm so glad. The young man said it would be, of course, but I've completely lost track of time, and—" She stopped, aware that her interrogator was waiting patiently for her to finish. "I'm sorry," she said. "I hope I didn't break any law?"

He looked as if he were seated at a garden party balancing a cup of tea on his knees instead of a notebook but his eyes were very watchful. "This man John Sebastian Farrell." He pronounced the name precisely and carefully. "You know this person?"

She nodded. "Yes, of course, or rather I used to. I'm trying to find him. You haven't—haven't come to tell me where he is, have you?"

"No, madam."

"For that matter," she added thoughtfully, "my name wasn't mentioned in the advertisement at all."

"The *Times* office gave me your name, madam, after which I contacted the tourist bureau to learn your itinerary. Now this man," he continued, courteous but resolute. "What causes you to believe he is in Zambia?"

Mrs. Pollifax started to reply and then stopped, suddenly anxious. "Is there something wrong? I don't understand—"

"If you will just answer—"

"Yes, of course," she said. "A mutual friend told me that he's living in Zambia and that he receives his mail in care of Barclay's Bank in Lusaka. I looked first in the telephone directory, but since his name wasn't listed I went to Barclay's Bank, where they told me his mail is collected very seldom and they had no forwarding address for him. So I thought of advertising." She paused, waiting, while he wrote this down. "Why?" she asked. "You surely haven't driven all the way from Lusaka to—"

"May I ask the name of your friend?"

"Friend?" she repeated blankly. "You can't possibly mean—"

"The mutual friend who told you this man lives in Zambia."

This sounded serious indeed. She said after a moment's hesitation, "Bishop. William Bishop."

"His address, please?"

"*Bishop's* address?" She was astonished but struggled gamely to remember where she sent Bishop's Christmas card. "Georgetown, in the District of Columbia," she said at last. "The Laurel Apartments, I believe. In the United States."

"Thank you," he said.

"And now that I've told you all this," she said firmly, "you will tell me, please, why it's so important?"

He put down his pen and folded away his notebook. "You are aware, madam, that you register and show your passport everywhere you go, so that no one may enter this country illegally."

"But I didn't enter—" She stopped in dismay. "You mean Mr. Farrell may be in your country illegally?"

"I did not say that, madam," he said politely. "I am checking into this matter."

"I see," she said, and then added accusingly, "Farrell is a very fine man, Lieutenant—"

"Lieutenant Bwanausi. Dunduzu Bwanausi."

"Lieutenant Bwanausi," she repeated bravely, and won a faint smile from him; in fact, he looked considerably friendlier as he rose from his chair. "That is quite possible, madam. We will see. I hope you enjoy your safari. Good day, madam."

She watched him go, her face troubled as she thought of the long dusty trip he had made here from Lusaka, and the long dusty trip back; it certainly did not imply any casual interest in Farrell. She felt, too, that there was something that she had missed during the interview, something wrong about it that she couldn't put her finger on. She sat and tried to reconstruct the interview.

A flock of tiny brilliant birds pecked at the earth around her. She heard the palms behind her stir once, convulsively, and then the sound of the launch starting up, followed by the steady putt-putt of its motor as it

backed and headed downriver to return Lieutenant Bwanausi to his car. The sun was growing intense on the
back of her neck, the air was dead-calm with a complete
absence of wind or breeze.

There was no breeze, she thought, and yet the palms
had rattled stridently a moment or two ago, a fact that
her mind had registered without her being aware of it.
Very odd, she decided, and swiftly, soundlessly left her
chair. The palms were silent now, and quite empty. She
moved in among them listening to the sound made as her
shoulders brushed against the brittle dry fronds. She tried
tapping a single branch with her fingers to see if a small
bird or animal could have rustled them, but she found
this quite impossible; someone human had to have dis-
turbed the palms to make the sound she'd heard, someone
standing and listening to Lieutenant Bwanausi.

She pushed through the bushes and out to the earthen
path behind them and looked toward the dining hall. The
distance was not far, and anyone could have reached it
from this point in a matter of seconds. There was no one
in sight. Walking quickly she passed the office and saw
Mrs. Lovecraft leaning over the desk talking animatedly
with Julian; she continued through the bar to the dining
room and counted heads: the rest of the party were
seated there waiting for lunch, relaxed, sprawling in their
chairs, laughing at something Chanda had said.

She withdrew before she could be noticed, realizing
that it could have been any one of them. It could have
been Cyrus Reed, who seemed to be keeping a very firm
eye on her, or it could have been Amy Lovecraft, who
had already ferreted out something to gossip about in
McIntosh. But Amy so much preferred males that it was

difficult for Mrs. Pollifax to imagine her curiosity extending to any female in the party.

Or it could, she reflected, have been the one person among them who would find the arrival of a policeman disturbing: *Aristotle*.

She did not like this thought. Remembering they were to leave for Kafwala immediately after lunch, she turned and hurried up the path to Leopard cabin to finish packing her suitcase.

CHAPTER
7

"The *mwamfuli* I could carry," Chanda said as Mrs. Pollifax prepared to board the pontoon boat after lunch.

Mrs. Pollifax was about to say that one multicolored parasol was no bother at all for her, but seeing the look on Chanda's face she promptly handed it over to him, and then demonstrated how it worked. The pontoon boat set off with them once again sitting on packing-cases, but Chanda made the trip standing in the bow under her umbrella, a broad grin on his face.

There were three Land Rovers waiting for them when they reached shore. Mrs. Pollifax, who had not yet considered the logistics of supplying a safari, stood and watched as their luggage was piled into one of the Land Rovers, followed by a sack of potatoes, a huge bag of green beans, two cases of beer and an insulated box filled to the brim with frozen chickens and steaks.

"Looks as if we'll eat well," Mr. Kleiber said in a pleased voice.

"Yes, doesn't it?" said Mrs. Pollifax, and recognizing the moment as an auspicious one—they were all standing in clusters watching—she lifted her camera and took a close-up picture of Mr. Kleiber.

"My yogurt lunches back home seem pathetic here," Lisa told Dr. Henry, and Mrs. Pollifax snapped a picture of them too, smiling at each other in the sun.

It was not the first time that she had noticed them smiling at each other. It had happened during the trip upriver this morning, and again at lunch, yet so far as she knew Lisa and Dr. Henry had exchanged no more than a few pleasantries, and Lisa was nearly always in the company of John Steeves, who seemed quite stricken by her. Mrs. Pollifax waited now for Tom Henry's response to this remark. He said, "Yes," and continued looking at Lisa until her smile deepened and she turned away—as if, thought Mrs. Pollifax, an entire conversation had just passed between them.

"I hope you're going to take my picture too," said Steeves.

"Oh, especially yours," Mrs. Pollifax told him, hating herself for gushing, "because my children will be so thrilled." She was conscious as she said this of Cyrus Reed turning and observing her with some astonishment. Really, she thought, Mr. Reed's attention, or rather his expectations of her, were going to prove extremely difficult on this trip. In a spirit of defiance she pointed her camera at him and took his picture too. She was completing her collection with a snapshot of Julian standing beside the Land Rover when he gestured to her to climb inside.

"You'll ride with me," he said, and helped her to climb up to the front seat.

She was joined almost immediately by a guard with a long rifle, the same guard who had opened the gate for them the day before, lean and graceful, dressed in khaki shorts and the same moth-eaten gray sweater. Then Lisa strolled over, followed by John Steeves, McIntosh and Amy Lovecraft. The Land Rover with their luggage had already started; Julian shouted at Crispin, climbed in, waved, and they too were off, leaving the others still arranging themselves in the third vehicle.

"Will they have a guard too?" asked Mrs. Pollifax.

Julian turned and looked at her with amusement. "Yes, of course. You still do not believe?"

Lisa leaned over and said, "Well, it *is* a park."

"I've heard," said Mrs. Lovecraft, "that Americans are accustomed to feeding the animals."

Julian grinned and shook his head. "It is safe most of the time so long as one remains on the roads, and in daylight, but even on the road—one of the guides at Luangwa Park was driving along like this three years ago when he was charged by a wounded buffalo. There was not much left of the Land Rover, I can tell you, and if the buffalo had not been quickly shot by the guard there would have been not much left of my friend either."

"I see," said Mrs. Pollifax, blinking. "What—uh—happens if you do have an emergency out here in the bush?"

"Oh, we have marconis," he explained, deftly steering

the car around a hole. "At Chunga there is a first-aid station too."

"Marconis?"

"Radio. Already this morning guests have used it. You sent a message to Lusaka, didn't you, Mrs. Lovecraft?"

"Yes," she said curtly.

"I did too," volunteered McIntosh.

"And if there is a serious emergency a Flying Doctor comes, but with Doctor Henry here—"

"*Nyalugwe*," said the guard sharply, and Julian braked.

"He says 'leopard.'" Julian stopped the Land Rover, and the only sounds were of McIntosh and Amy Lovecraft bringing out cameras and checking them; Mrs. Pollifax already held hers in her lap.

"There," said Julian, pointing, and on the crest of a small hill they saw a leopard standing in a tangle of thorn bush, his spots melting perfectly into the background. He turned and looked at them for a long moment, and then he lifted his magnificent blond head and walked away into the bush.

"My God how beautiful," whispered Lisa. "When you think that some silly woman would turn that fabulous creature into a fur coat—"

"Thank heaven for game parks," said Mrs. Pollifax. "Did you see his eyes, did you see those muscles when he moved?"

"Splendid specimen," said Steeves. "I've seen panthers before but never a leopard walking free."

"I believe I caught him on film," McIntosh said with satisfaction.

"Me, too," added Mrs. Lovecraft. "Thrilling."

"I missed," said Mrs. Pollifax sadly. "I was too busy looking."

They drove on along the dusty, shadeless road, of necessity driving slowly. Ahead of them a dozen black-and-white pin-striped fowl broke into a hurried trot. "Guinea fowl," said Julian, and honked the horn, which only caused the guinea fowl to scurry faster, their plump rear-ends registering their indignation until a second beep from the horn persuaded them to the right, and off the road. The Land Rover did not stop again, and as the road grew bumpier the interior of the car grew warmer; the guard in the rear slapped uninhibitedly at tse-tse flies and no one spoke. They came eventually to an inter-section marked *Kafwala 11 km.* and headed down a new dirt road. Its surface was dotted with elephant droppings, and the Land Rover rattled ominously as it hit the holes left by their crossing during the rainy season. The terrain was becoming heavily wooded now, with trees on either side of the road.

It was nearing three o'clock when they reached Kaf-wala, entering it from the rear where a man stood patiently ironing clothes on a slab of wood with a heavy old-fashioned iron. Half a dozen men lazed around a fire watching him and talking; they looked up eagerly at the sound of the Land Rover, which bumped past them and came to a halt in the middle of a grassy compound en-circled by tents and white cement huts with thatched roofs. Directly ahead of them stood a long white building with an arcade in its center; beyond it the earth sloped sharply down to the river. As soon as Julian cut the engine Mrs. Pollifax could hear the sound of rapids.

"This is Kafwala," announced Julian, and jumped down

from the Land Rover. "Here we stay for two days, game-viewing, before driving north to Moshe."

"Now this looks like a real camp," said Lisa with satisfaction. "Primitive. I think I'm going to like Kafwala very much." She turned and gave Mrs. Pollifax a hand. "Can you still walk? I feel as if I've been massaged all over. Crispin said there's a bathtub here, can you imagine? How on earth do you suppose they manage it?"

"They manage it," said Mrs. Lovecraft, climbing down, "by heating the water in a Rhodesian oven." She glanced around and pointed. "There it is, do you see? There's a drum of water inside that huge square of cement, they light a fire under it and the pipes carry the hot water to the tub or shower."

"Damned ingenious," murmured McIntosh. "I'll have to take a look at that."

"Yes, but how do you know such things?" asked Lisa.

"Oh my dear," she said in her slightly nasal voice, "I'm what you'd call a Colonial, I've lived in Africa all my life. In the Sudan, in South Africa, in Zambia, in Kenya."

Mrs. Pollifax looked at her with interest; she thought this explained her air of being British without being English. "Army?"

Mrs. Lovecraft turned and looked at her. "My father, yes. Not my husband. We had a tobacco farm until his death. Not far from here, farther south."

"I'm sorry."

"Oh—sorry," said Mrs. Lovecraft, and a scornful, bitter look crossed her face. "But you're a widow, too, aren't you?" She turned away abruptly and smiled at McIntosh. "I'm ready for a drink, ducks, aren't you?"

The Land Rover carrying their luggage bumped its way into camp and the Zambians surrounded it, laughing. Julian waved and then turned to Mrs. Pollifax. "Let me show you your room," he said, leading her toward the arcade set into the center of the long building. "Here," he said, pointing to a door set into the passageway, and then throwing open the opposite door he gestured to Lisa. "You and your father will be here, across from Mrs. Pollifax. Tea is at four, ladies," and with this he hurried off to distribute the others.

Lisa said, "Care for a look at the river?"

Mrs. Pollifax had opened the door to her room— there were no locks or keys—and was peering inside. It was dim because of the tall trees surrounding the building, but she saw the usual two beds shrouded in netting with a chamber-pot under each, a nightstand with a candle, but, most delightful of all, frosted glass windows and thick white walls. There would be no rustling noises tonight.

"A bit dark but very snug," said Lisa, looking over her shoulder. "I wonder if you'll have a roommate?"

"There's only Mrs. Lovecraft," pointed out Mrs. Pollifax.

She and Lisa exchanged a doubtful glance and Lisa laughed. "She's rather awful, isn't she? All that jewelry and pseudo-helplessness but under the fluff I'm beginning to sense the iron-hand-in-the-velvet-glove syndrome. My father had the effrontery to tell me last night that I'll end up just like her if I'm not careful."

"Now, that," said Mrs. Pollifax firmly, "is utterly impossible."

Lisa laughed. "That's because you didn't meet me in

my executive phase. I've really been quite a trial to Dad, I confess. He's an absolute dear but a great worrier. Heaven knows I've given him cause, though. There was a man, you see, and until he decamped I thought he'd solve all my problems."

"As no man can, of course," said Mrs. Pollifax.

Lisa nodded. "Yes, I see that now but for a long time I blamed myself, I felt so—so unlovable, you know? So I went to the opposite extreme and—and amputated every emotion that bubbled up, but of course that was ridiculous. It's taken me forever to understand that I'm still myself, and really a rather nice person, and that I just picked a lemon. I'm glad now," she said, smiling warmly at Mrs. Pollifax. "I don't know why I'm telling you all this—probably because I'll burst if I don't tell someone, and you look so—so human—but Africa's having the most tremendous impact on me. Ever since we arrived I've been having the strangest dreams at night, and seeing life and myself in the most astonishing perspective. This country's returning me to something I lost, it's disinhibiting me. Do you find this alarming?"

"No," said Mrs. Pollifax, smiling as she considered it. "No, because I've been here just long enough to see what you mean. Time seems very different here, as if it stopped and has only just begun again, and everything's new. And yet at the same time it's very old, pre-Biblically old, as if the world itself began here." She stopped and laughed. "Obviously I can't put it into words."

"One can't," Lisa said eagerly as they began walking down the path to the river under huge, ancient trees. "Not important emotions. And yet, you know, under the surface there seems to be a great deal going on here.

I had a very spooky thing happen to me yesterday when I was driving back to Lusaka. I thought I'd deliver this woman and her child directly to their village, which was about a mile off the main road, but after dropping them off I must have made a wrong turn because I couldn't find my way back, not even to her village." She paused and added with a shiver, "I kept driving until I was really lost, and then I came to a road-block on this dusty, deserted road and—really it was terrifying—I was suddenly surrounded by soldiers or police, I don't know which they were."

"Good heavens," said Mrs. Pollifax, startled.

Lisa nodded. "About twenty of them, all with rifles. They were terribly nice but at the same time they checked everything, my passport and visa, my luggage, the car. They must have kept me there for nearly an hour answering questions: why I was on that road, and where I was going, where I'd been, how long I was to be in Zambia and why I'd come to Zambia in the first place."

"Where did this happen?" asked Mrs. Pollifax.

Lisa frowned. "Somewhere down in the Kafue Flats area—that's what the map said, anyway."

"The driver who brought us to Chunga," said Mrs. Pollifax, "spoke of spies—Rhodesian spies—infiltrating Zambia."

"Probably," said Lisa. "There have been guerilla raids all along the Rhodesian border—except Africans call it Zambabwe, you know—and deep inside the country too. Not by Zambians but by revolutionaries crossing through Zambia, so I suppose the Rhodesians send people into this country as well. But if I lived next door to an *apartheid* country," she said hotly, "I don't think I'd sit on my hands either. I think it's terribly unfair that a minority of two hundred and fifty thousand white people have absolute power over six million natives and *squash* them. After all, it's their country."

"In general," said Mrs. Pollifax mildly, "the Golden Rule seems to be the last rule applied to any situation these days." They had reached the riverbank and she thought how incongruous it was to speak of violence in such a setting. On their left the water raced over great primeval boulders, shooting up plumes of spray and caressing the ear with its stormy descent. Once beyond the rocks the water gentled, sending small ripples to the shore at their feet until on their right it flowed smoothly around an island and became almost a backwash before it continued on its way south, to Chunga camp and beyond. There were several rough chairs placed near the bank, and a circle of them at the empty campfire site. "Rhodesia *is* very near," she said, sitting down in one of the chairs, "and Zambia used to be Northern Rhodesia, didn't it?"

"Oh yes," said Lisa, "but until you've visited Livingstone you've no idea *how* near. Half of Victoria Falls is in Rhodesia. I took one of those sundown cruises out of Livingstone, and one side of the river was Zambian and the other Rhodesian. The guide said we were under observation the entire time, because the river's the only barrier, and people can cross at night. In fact—"

She stopped as a voice hailed them from the top of the hill: the third Land Rover had arrived and John Steeves was descending, followed by Amy Lovecraft, Dr. Henry and—very gingerly—Willem Kleiber. A multicolored parasol next came into view, with Chanda under it. A moment later Cyrus Reed and McIntosh began descending the hill too, as well as a young man wearing a white linen jacket and carrying a tray of glasses.

Dr. Henry sat down near Lisa and smiled at her. "We saw a water buffalo, a number of puku and some impala."

She said, "We saw a leopard."

"I think," said John Steeves, taking the chair next to her, "that if you look very quickly into those palms to your left you can add a monkey to your list."

"Never mind the monkey," said Amy Lovecraft deflatingly. "Mrs. Pollifax, Julian asked me to tell you there's hot water now, and because there are so many of us we have to stagger our baths."

"And he's giving me first crack?" said Mrs. Pollifax. "Except I haven't the faintest idea where the bath is."

Chanda looked up and said eagerly, "I know where the *bafa* is, I will show you."

"Good, let's go," she told him, and rose from her chair to follow him up the hill. He chose to ignore the path and to leap gracefully from rock to rock, and for the first time she noticed the long puckered seam of a scar that ran up the back of his leg from the ankle to his thigh. She remembered Dr. Henry saying that he'd been nearly dead when he was brought into the hospital, and she wondered how many more scars there were. At the top of the hill he turned and waited for her, his eyes as luminous as if incandescent bulbs shone behind them.

"I move fast, like monkey," he said, grinning.

"You certainly do." Pausing to catch her breath she noticed a small chamois bag suspended about his neck on a string. "What's that, Chanda?" she asked, pointing.

He looked down in surprise, stuffed the bag quickly

inside his shirt again and gave her a thoughtful look. "*Cumo*," he said guardedly. Suddenly his enormous smile was back. "You like to see? It is my treasure."

"Love to," she told him. "Is it secret?"

"Very secret," he said, and seemed grateful when she opened the door of her room and beckoned him inside. First he gravely returned her parasol to her. "*Santi mukwai*," he said, and then he removed the chamois bag from around his neck and knelt beside her bed to empty its contents across the blanket.

She found herself both touched and amused at what emerged, remembering her son Roger's similar collection at this age, except that a more sophisticated society had rendered Roger's treasures obsolete. In the bush, Chanda's collection still had immediate value.

"From *cifulo*," Chanda said, pointing past the wall of her hut. "*Mushi*. My home."

"Do you mean your home before you met Dr. Henry?"

"Before this," he said, pointing matter-of-factly to his scarred leg, and picking up objects from his collection he explained them one by one. "*Munga*—thorn," he said.

"*Munga*," she repeated, nodding.

"*Bulobo*—fishhook. *Mwele*—knife." *Mwando* was a ball of string. *Lino* was a tooth—his own, she suspected, although his were white and gleaming. "And *cibiliti*," he added, holding up two safety matches.

"Yes, and a snake," she added, pointing to a dried skin.

"*Nsoka*," he said, smiling and nodding. "My father give me *nsoka*. He was hunter, very big man. He track game—*Ishanda Ionshe nama*. He teach me."

"So you'll be a hunter too?"

"Already a hunter," he said, grinning. "Very good one." She watched in silence as he returned his treasure to the chamois bag, his touch loving.

When he stood up she said quietly, "Thank you, Chanda."

"You *nunandi* now," he told her. "Friend. You and Dr. Henry. And now you have *bafa*," he said with his charming smile. "I show you."

Ten minutes later Mrs. Pollifax was seated in a hot tub in a small thatched hut, contentedly humming a song and reflecting that she was having a very good time on her safari and taking some very good pictures. Twenty minutes later, dressed again, she returned to her room and sat down on her bed to do a little planning about those pictures. Yesterday, for instance, she had completed her first film, tucked away now in her suitcase, and this morning she'd begun her second. That left four untouched cartridges, which meant—she made rapid mathematical computations—ninety-three more snapshots, many of which would have to be spent on animals and scenery. She was quite certain, however, that she'd already captured each of her traveling companions at least once on film, and this pleased her very much. Some of the pictures might not come out well, of course, but statistically it was a good beginning, and she thought that by tomorrow she could relax and become more casual about her filming. She happily touched the four sealed yellow boxes of film lined up in her suitcase and then she slipped her hand into the pocket of her folded bush jacket to check the completed cartridge she'd packed away this morning.

The cartridge wasn't there.

Startled, Mrs. Pollifax picked up the jacket, turned

each pocket inside out, shook the garment, tossed it
across the bed and began digging through her suitcase.
She could find no metal cartridge. She crawled under
the bed and searched and then checked through her purse:
no film. Thoroughly alarmed now, she picked up her
suitcase and dumped the contents all over the bed and
began a frenzied hunt.

Still there was no cartridge. Be calm, she thought, and
sat down on the bed in the middle of bright sweaters,
cold creams, slacks and sneakers, but there was no evading
the fact that the film was missing. Yet she'd packed it this
noon at Chunga camp before coming here, and several
minutes later when the boy had come for her suitcase
she'd reopened the bag to add her toothbrush, and the
exposed film had still been there: she could see it now
in her memory, sticking out of the pocket of her folded
bush jacket. And since her suitcase had been locked during its journey to Kafwala there could have been no
accident that would jar open the suitcase and scatter its
contents. The film had been locked inside her suitcase
when it left Chunga, and her suitcase had remained locked
until she had opened it half an hour ago to extract a bar
of soap for her bath. She'd reached inside without looking
because she knew exactly where the soap was, but she'd
had to unlock the suitcase to do so, and the lock had
not been tampered with then . . .

But if the film wasn't lost—and it couldn't have been,
she thought grimly, going over and over it—then it had to
have been stolen, and stolen while she was taking a bath.

She sat without moving, allowing the shock of this to
catch up with her, and it was a very real shock, with
implications that left her a little dizzy. How frightfully

arrogant she'd been, she thought, dashing about taking her snapshots so openly while all the time someone on this safari didn't want to be photographed. Someone had allowed her to snap as many of them as she pleased, and then her film had been quietly taken away from her. She had been discreetly and firmly put in her place.

Score one for Aristotle, she thought.

Brazen, of course, but so easy . . . an empty room with only an inside bolt on the door and no way of locking it on the outside, her suitcase unlocked and she in the bath- tub . . .

A flicker of anger stirred in her, grew, and at last tri- umphed over her alarm: it appeared that she now had a definite adversary, faceless, nameless and observant. She could assume that her burglar knew nothing about her except that she preferred faces mixed in with her scenery, but her unknown antagonist was clever, she knew that now. He had moved in early, counting on her not noticing, counting on her being a dithery, rather silly woman addicted to snapshots. He would do better next time, she thought, to leave an unexposed film behind him, because even silly dithery women noticed when too many exposed films disappeared.

But in the meantime she had lost twenty valuable pic- tures, and unless she could outthink her burglar she was doomed to see her completed films picked off like flies. It was also disturbing to realize that her collection was reduced to the six or seven snapshots still in her camera . . . or had these been tampered with too? The camera still registered seven snapshots on its gauge, and the cartridge looked untouched, but just to be certain she removed the film, put in a fresh one and dropped the half-completed one in her purse. The sealed boxes she hid: one in her totebag, one in the toe of a sneaker, the last inside her purse.

Defiantly she decided that she would continue her snap-shot-taking with an enthusiasm certain to annoy her adversary, but it was time now to turn to her lapel-pin camera. She had worn the latter pinned to her sweater and by now her companions must be accustomed to seeing her wear it, incongruous as it looked with casual clothes. She would continue to wear it doggedly.

Still shaken by her discovery she repacked her suitcase and locked it. As she left her room she found Cyrus Reed opening the door of the room on the other side of the arcade. He turned, looking genuinely surprised. "You're there?" he said. "Good, we're neighbors."

Even if it was he who had stolen her film, she thought it might be wise to mention her discovery of its disappearance. "If you've been down by the river," she said, "I wonder if you could tell me—or remember—just who left the group to walk up this way past my room?"

Reed looked from her to the door behind her and his brows lifted. "Something missing?" he asked quietly.

She nodded. "Yes, while I was in that building over there taking a bath. But I don't," she added, "want to cause a fuss."

"Quite right," he said. "Very sensible. And you want to know who left the party . . . Have to say nearly every-one," he said regretfully. "Let's see . . . good lord, even I left. Spilled some beer on my slacks, came up to change. Steeves ran out of film—passed him coming up as I went back. McIntosh left to take a nap—still gone. Kleiber came up for a map to prove some point or other, Lisa for a sweater. Chanda went with you and didn't return. Yes, I'd say the only two who stayed by the river were Mrs. Lovecraft and Dr. Henry. Nothing too valuable, I hope?"

"Fairly so, yes. To me."

"Don't like to hear that. You gave a thorough search? But of course you would." He placed the emphasis on *you* very flatteringly.

She gave him a smile and took a few steps toward the path. "A very efficient list, Mr. Reed. Thank you."

"No," he said firmly.

She turned in surprise.

"*Not* Mr. Reed. Call me Cyrus."

"Oh." She hesitated and then nodded. "And my name's Emily." As she descended the hill, leaving him behind, she realized that she felt obscurely better and was even smiling. A rather fatuous smile, she guessed, but still she was smiling.

By half-past six there was a crackling fire down by the river, the sole illumination except for a lantern hung from a post. They sat in a circle around the fire, drawn closer by the darkness beyond them and by the feeling of being very small under the huge trees and beside the roaring river. They sat and talked and sipped beer. The only activity came from two people: one the grave-faced young man in a white jacket who came down the hill bearing silverware, napkins and plates, then went up again and returned with cups and saucers, more beer and glassware. The other was Mrs. Pollifax who, with a flashcube attached to her camera, knelt, hovered, stood, sat and wickedly took picture after picture.

"Why do you bother," asked Mr. Kleiber curiously, "when you don't have a good German camera like Mr. McIntosh or Mrs. Lovecraft?"

"Oh, but this camera is just fine for an amateur," she said. "I snap pictures just for my children, you know. They'll be fascinated, and then of course my grandchildren will love seeing the animals. I always try," she told him firmly, "to create a total background, so that they can step into the adventure and experience it too."

"And do you," asked Cyrus Reed dryly, "show slides?"

She gave him a level glance and without batting an eyelash, for she loathed slides, said, "Of course."

"Incredible," he said, staring at her.

On an inspired note she added, "As a matter of fact after dinner I'll bring down pictures of my grandchildren to show you. They're very *lovely* grandchildren."

"Really?" said Amy Lovecraft coldly.

The young waiter had just arrived bearing a large tray, followed by two young men carrying steaming dishes, and he chose this moment to announce that dinner was served. Mrs. Pollifax jumped up immediately and became the first to approach the food spread out on the table. She was not surprised when she returned to her chair to find herself something of a pariah after her announcement about snapshots. Mr. Kleiber chose a seat as far removed from her as possible, and Mrs. Lovecraft, who had shown no real interest in Mr. Kleiber before, eagerly took the chair next him. Lisa, assuming a more neutral corner, was joined by Steeves as usual. Tom Henry found a seat not far from Lisa, and McIntosh, still smiling enigmatically, sat beside Julian.

Only Chanda and Cyrus Reed showed signs of not

being infected. Chanda sat down cross-legged on the ground beside Mrs. Pollifax and gave her a dazzling white smile. "I sit here. You *nunandi.*"

"Damn awkward eating from one's lap," growled Reed.

"Try a corner of this little table," suggested Mrs. Pollifax. "After all, the word safari means camping."

"*Touché,*" he said, smiling. "Thanks. Incredibly good food. Can't imagine how they do such a *cordon bleu* job out here without electricity."

"There is big wood stove," Chanda told him eagerly, "and very fine cook. Julian calls him a—a chef."

Reed nodded. "That's it, then. Saw you up there poking around. Anyone else speak Bemba here?"

"*Cimo,*" said Chanda, holding up one finger. "There is good life here in park, maybe I not be hunter."

"Tom said you're damn good at hunting and tracking and only twelve years old," pointed out Reed, deftly spearing a piece of steak. "Said you went off to see what's left of your old village on the Angolan border this spring, and hiked fifty miles through the bush alone."

Chanda's smile deepened. "Yes, that. He tell you about the lions?"

"Lions!" exclaimed Mrs. Pollifax.

"Three of 'em," said Reed, nodding, "but how did you know they were following you, Chanda?"

"Because—" Chanda hesitated. "I do not know name for *cula.*"

Several chairs away, Julian said, "Frogs, Chanda."

"Ah! Yes. I hear them, you know. They make a frog sound, and then I cross *kamana*—"

"Brook," called Tom Henry.

"Yes, brook, and frogs are very noisy talking to each

other. I walk more, and then—" He lifted one hand and cut the air dramatically. "*Cula* sound stop. So I look for big tree to climb because it becomes dark, like now, and I know something follows me or the frogs would be making noise."

"Good heavens," said Lisa. They were all listening now.

"Three lions try to climb tree for me, but I am too high. I sit all night for them to go away."

"I take it they did eventually," said Steeves.

"But not until morning," put in Tom Henry.

"Yes, I climb down from tree but cannot walk. *Mwendo* become like tree too."

"He means he'd lost all circulation in his legs," explained Tom. "His limbs had become like the tree."

Chanda nodded. "So I hunt sticks and dry grass and after long time make fire rubbing sticks. This is very hard to do. For many hours I sit to warm myself at fire, and then I go."

"Something I can't imagine any American twelve-year-old doing," said Reed.

"Still, Africa's a shade more hospitable a country than Mongolia," put in Steeves. "There you've panthers and tigers, but even if the sun shines three hundred days a year you get tremendous winds and a horrendous wind-chill factor."

"Tigers we don't have," said Julian, "but tomorrow we look for lion for you."

"Oh, I do hope we see one," cried Lisa eagerly.

"What time do we start?" asked Mrs. Pollifax.

"Directly after breakfast, about half-past seven."

"Early," said Amy Lovecraft, making a face.

The white-jacketed waiter had brought down a new

tray which he set upon the table. Now he bowed, his face grave, and said, "Pudding is served, please, ladies and gentlemen."

It was after the pudding that Tom Henry reminded Chanda he was tired today and it was time for him to invest in some sleep. The boy arose from his cross-legged stance on the ground, and at the same moment Mrs. Pollifax had a sudden, dazzling idea. She, too, arose. "I'll go up with Chanda," she said. "It's so dark I couldn't bring myself to go alone, but if we're breakfasting at seven—"

"What, no snapshots of your grandchildren?" asked Reed mischievously.

"I'm still catching up on my sleep," she said, ignoring him and picking up her purse. "Good night!"

A chorus of farewells followed her as she turned away from the fire. It was very dark outside the circle of light and Chanda took her hand and guided her. Pebbles slid underfoot; the sound of the rushing water behind them made a low musical backdrop, rather soporific, she thought, like the murmur of voices heard from a distant room. There was a lantern waiting at the top of the hill, placed on a table in the center of the arcade. She turned and looked back at the campfire, counting heads. They were all there, no one had left. She said, "Chanda . . ."

"Yes, madam."

"Chanda, I wonder if you'd hide something for me— keep something for me—in your *cumo* bag."

He stared at her, eyes clouded now, opaque, mysterious, so that she wondered if he understood.

"It's something important and quite small. Only until

the safari ends," she added quickly. "It needs—needs hiding." She walked around the corner of the passageway out of the lantern's light and opened her camera and removed the film that she'd completed down by the campfire. When she held it out to Chanda he remained impassive, the expression in his eyes chilling, as if he looked into, through and beyond her into something she couldn't see. Then abruptly the mask splintered into smiles, the strange effect was gone and an enormous smile lighted up his eyes.

"Yes, secret," he said, nodding, and taking the cartridge from her hand he loosened the string of his chamois bag and dropped the film inside.

She realized that she had been holding her breath; she exhaled now in relief. "You're a real friend, Chanda."

"But of course—*nunandi*," he said, laughing, and raced off into the darkness, calling over his shoulder, "Good night, madam!"

She stared after him thoughtfully. She did hope he understood but at least in giving him one of her films she felt that she had diversified, and this lifted her spirits. Her glance moved to the fire at the rear of the camp where the silhouettes of half a dozen men crouched talking around the blaze. She turned to go to her room and jumped when she saw Cyrus Reed standing in the arcade watching her.

"Oh—you startled me," she gasped, and wondered how long he'd been standing there and how much he'd seen.

He held out her sun-goggles and her umbrella. "Left these behind you," he said, handing them to her, and then, "Care for a stroll around the compound before turning in?"

She hesitated. "I do feel rather unexercised," she admitted.

"Good. Damn good display of Orion and the Pleiades if we can get away from the light of the fire. Tiresome down below after you left. Can't help noticing that Mrs. Lovecraft talks through her nose and Mr. Kleiber sniffs a great deal through his, and Steeves was running on about Mongolia, which is all very well but this is Africa."

She laughed. "You poor man."

"Not at all," he said amiably, taking her arm. "Decided to look for better company."

"I think your daughter Lisa's a darling, by the way."

"She is, isn't she? Seems to be thawing out now. Damn glad to see it."

"And you," she said, "are really a judge?"

He brought out his flashlight, checked it and nodded. "A *phungu*, Julian tells me. The Nyanga word for judge or counselor."

"*Phungu*," she repeated, trying it out on the tongue. "Sounds a little like fungus. What sort of *phungu* were you before you retired? Did you have hundreds of exciting cases?"

"Strictly routine," he said, "except for the Rambeau-Jenkins case."

Mrs. Pollifax stopped in her tracks and stared at him. "Oh," she gasped, "do you think she murdered him?"

He had been staring up at the sky; now he turned and looked down at her and smiled his sleepy smile. "That, my dear, only God knows."

"But you were there, you presided, and I've so often wondered—"

"Ha—common fallacy, that," he told her. "We *phungus*

never judge guilt or innocence, we judge evidence. The law isn't emotional, you know, it's cold and impersonal. Has to be."

"But you're not," she told him indignantly.

She could see his smile in the light of the campfire. "Don't ever tell anyone, my dear." He stopped and said, "With you the 'my dear' just slips out."

"Well, *I* think Nina Rambeau was innocent," she said, and hoped he wouldn't notice that she was blushing. She wondered how long it had been since anyone had called her "my dear." "Have you found Orion yet?"

He shook his head. "Glow from the men's campfire bleaches out the stars. Daresay if we wandered a little way up the road we could see better."

"Oh, do let's," she said.

He nodded pleasantly to the men around the campfire as they passed. "Just looking at the stars," he told them, pointing at the sky.

The men burst into smiles and nods.

"Damn lot livelier up here than down by the river," he said mildly as they left the fire behind and entered the road beyond.

They had ventured a few paces into the darkness when Mrs. Pollifax looked back and sighed. "It's the guard," she told Reed. "He's *following* us, isn't that ridiculous?"

"Not at all," said Reed thoughtfully. "Can't have it both ways, my dear."

"Can't—what do you mean by that?"

"Well," he said in his mild voice, "if you want to ob-serve wild animals in perfect safety you capture them, bring 'em back to our world and look at them behind bars in a zoo. Here we're their guests," he pointed out.

"Trespassers, actually. They run free, wild and protected, but we do *not*."

"Of course you're right," she said reluctantly. "It's just that it's so *confining* not to be able to leave camp without being followed."

"Doubt if anyone could confine you, my dear. Ought to mind his presence far more than you since I've every intention of kissing you."

She turned and looked at him in astonishment, which placed her in the perfect position for him to make good his intention. "Orion be damned," he said, and swept her into his arms.

Mrs. Pollifax gave a small squeak of protest, resisted briefly and then discovered that she fitted very nicely into the curve of his arm and that she enjoyed being kissed very much. When he let her go she promptly dropped her sun-goggles, her kerchief and her umbrella. "Oh," she stammered. "Oh dear."

He patiently retrieved them and handed them back to her. "And there," he said, grasping her hand and firmly holding it in his, "is Orion."

"Yes," she said, feeling very disoriented and breathless as she realized that she was not immune, after all, to huge and charming *phungus*. It was all very disconcerting, she thought—at her age, too—and then she lifted her gaze to the sky and was struck breathless all over again. "Oh," she whispered.

It was like standing in the center of a planetarium, the sky a huge bowl turned upside down and fitted snugly to the horizon and then filled with thousands upon thousands of stars. This, surely, was infinity, she thought, gazing up in awe, and slowly became aware of the silence surrounding them, a silence like the beginning or the end of the world.

It was interrupted by a cough from the guard some distance behind them. Cyrus said dryly, "I think we're keeping him, he's been patient with us long enough."

Without speaking they turned and walked back to camp.

When Mrs. Pollifax entered her room again it was already very cold and she paused only long enough to slip a new cartridge of film into her camera and to hide the camera under her pillow for the night. Blowing out the candle beside her bed she inserted herself between the blankets, tucked the mosquito netting around her and was surprised to find her room still filled with light. She noticed now what had escaped her by daylight: the wall of the room over her door rose only to a height of eight feet. Between this and the inverted V of the rafters there was only mosquito netting, so that she could see the glow of the lantern in the passageway outside.

She lay gazing up at this light and thinking about her strange day, about her film being stolen and then about Cyrus Reed, who was proving very distracting indeed. She realized that she was going to have to discipline herself very severely; after all, for her this was no ordinary safari. She was here for a purpose, and if she was not attentive and very clever, then Aristotle would continue wandering around the world negotiating contracts to shoot more people and this would never do.

Never, she thought, and resolved to put Cyrus Reed completely out of her mind. She closed her eyes and then opened them when she heard voices and footsteps outside on the path. A moment later she recognized Amy Lovecraft's high-pitched laugh.

"I would have fallen, Mr. Kleiber, if you'd not rescued me like a knight in shining armor, you dear man. This path—"

Amy Lovecraft, thought Mrs. Pollifax, was definitely hunting something more than game.

"I do not understand," Mr. Kleiber said in his pedantic, humorless voice, "why one bulldozer could not be assigned to this hill. They have the bulldozers, I know. They use them on the roads, and with only one hour of work—"

"Are you in the construction business, Mr. Kleiber? You seem to know so much about machinery."

"Heavy machinery, yes. I sell worldwide. It's—"

Their voices blurred as they passed from the arcade into the compound; she heard one more brittle laugh pierce the stillness and then there was silence. Mrs. Pollifax had closed her eyes again when she heard fresh pebbles crunching underfoot outside the building. "Really beautiful," Lisa Reed was saying. "I love it, don't you?"

It was Tom Henry who replied. "Absolutely." A comfortable silence followed and then Tom said, "John Steeves is certainly very distinguished."

Lisa said carelessly, "Oh—distinguished, yes."

"As a matter of fact we've one of his paperbacks at the hospital. *One Hundred Nights in a Yurt*, I think. The chap who read it—"

"Tom."

"Mmmm?"

"Don't be a goose."

Tom Henry laughed. "Have a good sleep, my dear."

Mrs. Pollifax heard him walk away and Lisa open the door of the room opposite hers. A very interesting exchange of words, she thought, smiling, very interesting indeed, and wondered on whom she might eavesdrop next.

She was not kept waiting long: McIntosh came next through the arcade, talking to Cyrus, and for a man of smiling silence McIntosh had suddenly become very articulate. ". . . Monetary Fund, of course. You simply can't cure inflation unless nations stop going to the printing press. The world is being drowned in worthless paper . . . Irresponsible. Expedient, of course, but disastrous. No discipline without paper being backed by something."

"Gold?" inquired Cyrus.

"Probably, yes. We've not been on a gold standard since 1901. Governments sneer at it, of course, because it would force discipline on them. But mark my words, Reed, whole civilizations have become graveyards by corrupting their currency."

"You do considerable business between countries?"

"Oh yes, quite international, but of course multinational's the word these days. But I don't want to hold you up, we can continue this another time. Good night, Reed."

"Yes . . . Lions tomorrow. Good night."

The last to pass by her door were Julian and John Steeves, and they were walking much faster. ". . . oh, much better here," Julian was saying. "Too many young men of my country head for the cities, and this is bad. Lusaka is full of thieves and spies."

"Excellent sense," said Steeves. "I'm not very big on

cities myself. I like your bush, it has a mystique . . ."

Mrs. Pollifax did not hear the rest because they had
left the arcade and their voices faded. In any case she
was growing warmer now, and with this came a voluptu-
ous drowsiness: she closed her eyes and slept and
dreamed of masks. In her dream she sat in a theater and
one by one each member of the safari walked out on stage
to form a single line facing her. It was only when they
moved up to the footlights in unison that Mrs. Pollifax
saw they were holding masks to their faces. At a given
signal each mask was swept away, but underneath lay
another mask, and then another and still another . . .

CHAPTER

8

When Mrs. Pollifax woke at half-past six the next morning it was bone-chillingly cold. The young waiter who brought coffee to her room on a tray said, "Good morning, madam," and it was so cold that wisps of vapor curled from his lips to match the steam rising from the coffeepot. Mrs. Pollifax put one foot out of bed, poured coffee into a cup and carried it under the blankets with her, wondering if she would ever be warm again.

"I thought Africa was t-t-tropical," she protested at breakfast, which was served down by the river in the morning mist.

"We're four thousand feet above sea level," Julian reminded her with a flash of white teeth. "You are ready for lion? Perhaps it will warm you to hear that Crispin took the Land Rover out at dawn and found lion tracks six miles north of camp."

"Oh how wonderful!" gasped Mrs. Pollifax.

Almost as exciting was the news that overnight two of the Land Rover roofs had been removed so that they could ride standing up and scan the savannah for game, like professionals. Mrs. Pollifax could scarcely wait.

But in spite of her excitement she had not forgotten her resolve of the night before, and between breakfast and departure time she retired to her room to make a list for the day and contemplate it. *Find out*, she wrote, *who's traveled widely during the past eight months (France—Costa Rica).* To this she added: *Try McIntosh again, could be opening up. Mr. Kleiber: if good at machinery ask about guns. John Steeves: what disguises preferred?* She studied this memo and then lit a match and burned it.

They set out shortly afterward in the two Land Rovers, the sun higher now and promising warmth soon. For this excursion Mrs. Pollifax had arranged her clothing in layers so that as the day advanced she could remove first her bush jacket, and then her heavy sweater, and then the pale-blue cardigan until eventually—it was rather like peeling an artichoke, she thought—she would be resplendent in striped shirt and kerchief before the process reversed itself. She also carried her bright parasol and two rolls of film for her camera and wore her lapel pin.

As they left Kafwala camp behind and headed for the open savannah Mrs. Pollifax realized that, like Lisa, Africa was having its charismatic effect upon her: the road wound ahead of the Land Rover like textured brown ribbon, the high grass tawny on either side and the earth flat under the incredible arc of blue African sky. There were also the surreal notes: a candelabra tree, its limbs perfectly splayed, its blossoms a dull orange; a baobub tree smooth and silvery in the warm morning light, and when Mrs. Pollifax inquired of Julian what the cement posts along the road meant, Julian laughed. "Not cement —termite nests." Bringing the Land Rover to a halt he jumped out and kicked at the top one, exposing holes like a honeycomb.

It was Mrs. Pollifax who spotted the elephants first. "Oh look," she cried, and in both Land Rovers heads swiveled to the left. At some distance away from them a line of elephants was moving across the savannah, an entire family with three young ones among them.

"Baby *nsofu*," said Chanda, pointing and grinning.

"I count nine," volunteered Cyrus, standing beside her.

Mrs. Pollifax stood up on the seat and took three pictures in rapid succession, and then somewhat reluctantly slid down in the seat and snapped a close-up shot of John Steeves as he watched the procession.

"Can we get out?" called Amy Lovecraft, who was all beige and white today, with a green kerchief around her hair.

"Better if we drive ahead down the road," said Julian. "They're heading for water, we'll see them closer farther along."

The two Land Rovers inched ahead for half a mile and stopped, after which everyone climbed out and stood in a group waiting, cameras ready.

"This light," said Mrs. Pollifax, gesturing widely toward the sky. "It so reminds me of the light in southern

France. The same luminous quality. Has anyone been in France lately?"

No one appeared to pay her the slightest attention; John Steeves stared inscrutably into the distance; McIntosh was busy with his light meter; Mr. Kleiber grunted noncommittally, while Amy Lovecraft simply ignored her. Only Cyrus turned and looked at her. "No," he said. "Have you?"

Having never visited France in her life, Mrs. Pollifax found herself figuratively pinned to a wall and was happy to be rescued by the elephants. "Here they come," she cried.

The elephants emerged from a copse of trees and lumbered toward them, trunks swinging. They crossed the road only twenty feet away from them without so much as a glance at their audience. The baby elephants brought a laugh from Lisa. "They're *darling!*"

Satisfied, they climbed into the Land Rovers and drove on. Gradually the topography began to fold in upon itself, nurturing seams and hollows and small hills. The Land Rover coasted down an incline to a dried-up brook bed surrounded by tangles of thorn bush and twisted roots. It stopped and Julian climbed out. "Here," he called, beckoning, and when they joined him it was to see the imprint of a lion paw in the dust.

The Land Rovers drove ahead in low gear, no one speaking now. Cautiously they rounded a wide curve, slowed as they approached a grassless area beside the road, and—Mrs. Pollifax caught her breath in awe— there lay two lions stretched out sleeping in the sun. The Land Rover coasted to a stop only eight feet away from the lions; beside Mrs. Pollifax the guard leaned forward and swung his rifle into horizontal position, his eyes watchful.

"A lioness and a male," whispered Julian.

As the second Land Rover drew up behind them the lioness lifted her magnificent head, yawned and rose to her feet. She stretched, looked them over without interest and sniffed the air. The male stirred and rose to his feet too, massive, nearly nine feet in length, and Mrs. Pollifax held her breath as he stared unblinkingly at them. Remembering her camera just in time, she snapped a picture only a second before the two beautiful tawny creatures slipped away into the grass and vanished.

"Lion," breathed Mrs. Pollifax, and felt that her cup was full to the brim.

At noon they came to Lufupa camp, which was small —for weekend people only, Julian said—and not yet open for the season. The camp occupied a point of land where the Kafue River curved and broadened, smooth as a millpond in the noon sun. They were to lunch here, Julian said, pointing to a picnic table under the acacia trees.

Mrs. Pollifax had now removed three of her layers of clothing and was happy to sit in the shade. It was a tranquil scene: not far away two men were painting chairs a bright blue in the grass, and mattresses were being aired in the sun. Up on the roof of the largest hut an old man was spreading out fresh thatch and tying it down with wire, like shingles. Finding herself next to Mr. Kleiber at the picnic table, she turned to him with a warm smile. "Do you know much about guns, Mr. Kleiber? I'm wondering if you can tell me what sort of rifle our guard carries."

The man serving them their lunch chose this moment to place in front of Mr. Kleiber a plate of chicken, mashed potatoes, gravy and fresh tomatoes. McIntosh, seated across the table, answered instead. "A 3006, I'd say."

"Oh—you know guns," she said brightly.

"Or possibly a 3004," Kleiber said with his mouth full.

"A 3004," Crispin told them from the end of the table.

Very inconclusive, thought Mrs. Pollifax, and decided there was something far too relaxing about all this fresh air and that an evening campfire might be the better place for tactful interrogations.

After lunch they strolled upriver a short distance, with guards at their front and rear, and watched hippos bathing in the shallows. This especially pleased Cyrus because there had been no ox-peckers on the backs of the hippos they'd seen at Chunga camp.

"Ox-peckers?" echoed Mrs. Pollifax.

"Tick-birds," he explained, and pointed. "Find them on rhinos' backs too. Feed on their ticks and conveniently warn them of danger." His glance moved to John Steeves, who was helping Lisa remove her sweater, and he frowned. "Chap really seems to be zeroing in on Lisa. Very confidently too."

Mrs. Pollifax smiled. "If there's one thing John Steeves has, I'm sure it's confidence."

"Seems a decent enough chap," said Reed. "Just difficult to picture as a son-in-law. I mean—yurts?"

"Oh, I don't think you need worry about that."

"No?" said Reed, looking surprised. "Together all the time."

"There are," said Mrs. Pollifax, "undercurrents."

"I'm overlooking something?"

"You've been watching Steeves and not your daughter. He's with her, but she's not with him, if you follow me. It's a matter of the eyes. Glances."

"You astonish me," said Cyrus, and turning to her he added accusingly, "Matter of fact, you've astonished me ever since we met."

Mrs. Pollifax found herself blushing—really it was very tiresome, she'd not blushed in years—and fielded this statement by turning to Mr. Kleiber, who was looking distinctly bored by the hippos. "Still no crocodiles, Mr. Kleiber?"

He looked startled. "Not yet, no. Dear me, I hope soon, though. What a hot sun, I think I've had enough of walking."

She thought that Mr. Kleiber had begun thawing out a little today; the pinched look was no longer so pronounced, and occasionally he smiled at something said by the group. He appeared to like McIntosh, whose reticence matched his own, and when something unusual occurred he would look first to McIntosh, rock a little on his heels while he waited to catch his eye, and then deliver himself of a pithy comment in his dry, sarcastic voice. He had begun to tolerate Amy Lovecraft too, no longer looking frost-bitten when she took his arm and asked if he minded her walking with him.

"Crocodiles you will see at Moshe tomorrow," said Julian, overhearing him. "The camp is very open, right on the river, and the crocodiles sun themselves on the banks."

They turned to go back and Mrs. Pollifax fell into

step beside Cyrus. Never having walked behind Mr. Kleiber before, she was amused now to see what an odd
walk he had: a strut, she thought, with a stutter. He
walked with his shoulders rigid, back straight and head
high, but his right foot toed in slightly and threw the
rhythm just a shade off balance, like one instrument in a
band playing a beat behind the others.

"Looks like company up ahead," said Cyrus.

A shiny beige Land Rover was parked next to the safari
jeeps, and three men, all black, were talking to the
workmen. As they drew nearer, one of them climbed
back into the car and the other two could be seen
shaking hands and saying goodbye. The man in the car
leaned forward and gestured to them to hurry.

Reed said abruptly, "Chap on the left in the green
shirt is the man who was asking for you at the hotel. In
Lusaka, when I was checking out."

Startled, Mrs. Pollifax said, "Are you sure?"

"Never forget a face. Shall I give him a shout?"

"Oh yes, do," she said, hurrying.

Reed began to shout, and Mrs. Pollifax waved franti-
cally, but the two men gave them only a quick glance
and then jumped into the Land Rover and the car sped
away. A moment later it had vanished among the trees.

"Had his chance," said Cyrus. "Muffed it."

"But they must have heard you," protested Mrs. Pollifax, "and if they were deaf they would have seen me
waving, because they turned and looked."

Approaching the Lufupa workers Cyrus said, "From
the city, were they?"

"Oh yes, sir," the elder said, beaming. "They did not
know the camp is closed. Three gentlemen from Lusaka."

"Didn't they wonder what we're doing here?"

"Oh yes, missis. I told them you are all from Kafwala camp, on organized safari."

Odd, thought Mrs. Pollifax, frowning, very odd, and could not quite shrug off the sensation that if Cyrus was accurate, then forces were in motion that she did not understand. Turning to him she said stubbornly, "I don't —I really don't—see how on earth you can be so certain it was the same man."

"Could be wrong," he said fairly.

She looked at him quickly. "Are you often wrong?"

"No. Study too many faces in court. Habit of mine."

She nodded. Nevertheless he'd admitted that he could be wrong and she clung to this, because otherwise she was left with the uneasy mystery of a man who wanted to see her in Lusaka and then, catching up with her, jumped into a car to avoid being seen.

Some hours later Mrs. Pollifax, happily showering back at camp, was tempted to break into song again. Life in the bush, she thought, certainly stripped one of inconsequentials: she had been hot and dusty for hours and now the cold water splashing over her heated skin brought a delightful tingly sensation. She had been out-of-doors since dawn, and soon there would be a feast around the campfire for which she already had a ravenous appetite. She wondered when she had felt so free . . . perhaps never . . . and running through her mind like a melody were little vignettes of the road at midday: the hot sun, dust, the orange trunk of a thorn tree as well as another tree they'd seen bearing long torpedo-shaped gray fruit that Julian had called a sausage tree. She had also learned to say thank you in Nyanga—*zikomo kuambeia*—and at Lufupa . . .

But it was better not to think of Lufupa, she reminded herself. The memory of it raised disturbing questions because they set in motion doubts that eventually, no matter how she reasoned them away, returned full circle to Cyrus. It was Cyrus, after all, who had told her that a man had asked for her at the hotel after she had left, and it was Cyrus who insisted now that it was this same man they'd seen at Lufupa camp, but she had only his word for there being such a man at all. What was she to make of it? If Cyrus was Aristotle . . . she shivered at this demonic thought and turned off the water and reached for a towel. But if Cyrus was Aristotle, it didn't make sense his manufacturing a Mr. X who was looking for her, and if he had *not* fabricated this stranger—if there really was such a man . . .

"There you are!" said a man's voice suddenly, and Mrs. Pollifax jumped.

Outside the shower hut Lisa's voice replied. "Hello, John, I was just looking for a sunny spot to dry my hair."

"Where is everyone?"

"Oh—around." Lisa's voice was vague. "Mrs. Pollifax was waiting to take a shower when I came out but she's gone now. Dad and Chanda are over at the kitchen watching the chef start dinner on that funny stove they have here. Mr. Kleiber pricked a finger and Tom is assuring him that he's not going to get a rare African disease. McIntosh is napping and—"

"Enough, enough!" he said with mock despair. "What I really came to ask you is why you've been avoiding me since lunch. It made me wonder. Look here, was it a shock to you when I said I'd been married once, very briefly, years ago?"

"A shock? Good heavens, no, John!"

"What *did* you think?"

Mrs. Pollifax, torn between announcing herself and listening, opted for the latter and continued dressing.

"I thought," Lisa was saying slowly, "if I remember correctly, that I wasn't surprised it lasted only six months. I thought you must be a rather difficult person to be married to."

"A rather difficult—! And here I was hoping—what on earth makes you say that?"

"Well—there's something secret about you, isn't there, John? Something concealed, a little room somewhere marked 'Keep Out'?"

There was a long silence and then Steeves said lightly, "This is rather a setback for me, Lisa, I was hoping to ask you to marry me when the safari ends."

"Me?"

"Did you really think I went about squiring beautiful young girls so attentively every day?"

"No—that is, surely you were just being friendly? John, I'm terribly flattered but let's not talk about this any more. We shouldn't do at all, you know."

"Why wouldn't we 'do at all,' as you put it?"

"Because . . . well, you don't really have room in your life for marriage, do you?"

"I could change, you know," he said. "I don't have to go batting around the world forever."

"Change into what?" she asked, and then, indignantly, "And why should you? You're a beautiful person, John, just as you are. You give a great many people pleasure

by doing all the wonderfully dashing things they day-
dream of doing. It's marvelous."

"And very lonely," he pointed out.

At this moment Mrs. Pollifax decided that it was more
than time to announce herself: she dropped her shoe on
the cement slab and said, "Oh dear!" and continued
dropping things and picking them up again to give Lisa
and Steeves time to adjust to her presence. When she
walked out of the shower hut John had vanished and
Lisa was folding up her chair. She turned and smiled
faintly. "I suppose you heard all?"

"It was impossible not to," admitted Mrs. Pollifax. "I
waited as long as I could, but it was growing very damp
and cold in there. It's nearing sunset time, I think."

"Yes, time for sweaters again. Thank you for—well,
rescuing me." She fell into step beside her, absently
carrying the chair along with her. "Isn't life strange?"
she asked. "I read John's latest book this winter and his
photograph occupied the entire back of the bookjacket
and I used to look at it—those sad eyes practically
stabbing my soul—and I'd say, 'Now there's a man, if only
I could meet someone like that.' "

"And now you have," said Mrs. Pollifax, giving her an
interested glance, "and you find a room inside of him
marked 'Keep Out'?"

"You really did hear everything." Lisa sighed. "I wonder what made me say that. John strikes me—now that
I've met him—as a character in a very contemporary
novel, the kind that begins and ends in the same way,
with the hero staring into his scotch and soda and about
to leave another woman behind as he goes off to a new

adventure. He seems—caught by something. And terribly sad about it."

"Caught," repeated Mrs. Pollifax musingly. "A strange word to use."

"People do get trapped, I suppose. Inside of images, all kinds of things. But he is a lovely person, isn't he?"

Mrs. Pollifax nodded. "A very unusual man, yes, very charming and—as you suspected—very much a loner. But I think you're looking for someone a little cozier, aren't you?"

Lisa burst out laughing. "Cozier?"

"Someone warm and caring and devoted. Less complicated." She reached her door and opened it. "It is sometimes," she said, "very difficult to remain faithful to *oneself*."

"Oh, I do hope you like Dad as much as he likes you," Lisa blurted out, and then stopped, blushing. "Oh dear, I didn't mean—What on earth am I doing carrying this chair with me?" she asked, noticing it for the first time. "I really must change for dinner. Which in this case," she added, laughing, "means removing one sweater and adding another, or changing from jeans to corduroys!"

The sun had already set when Mrs. Pollifax descended the hill to join the group around the campfire, and the single lantern hanging from the post had been lighted. The flames of the fire held shades of blue in them tonight, and the wood crackled merrily.

"You mised an egret," Cyrus told her with a welcoming smile. "Incredible sight."

"And a family of monkeys scolding us from the trees," put in Tom Henry. "They were certainly cross at finding us here again, this must be their playground."

"A dozen at least," added Lisa.

"God I'm hungry," said Amy Lovecraft. She was wearing still another new outfit tonight, a blue Jacquard turtleneck and dark-blue slacks over which she'd thrown a fleecy red jacket. Mrs. Pollifax wondered how many suitcases she traveled with, and decided it was better not to know.

Julian said, "I've given orders that dinner be served early tonight—before seven—because everyone is so hungry."

"Marvelous," said Amy, pronouncing it mav-lus.

"And what time is it now?"

Julian glanced at his watch and frowned. "The men are late, they should have begun setting the table by now. I'd better go up and see what the matter is."

"Yes, do," said Amy. "Frankly we're all starving."

Julian half rose from his chair and then froze and fell back in astonishment. Following his gaze Mrs. Pollifax saw three men move out of the darkness toward the campfire, silently, like phantoms rising out of the mist. At first she didn't understand, thinking them Kafwala workers whom she'd not seen before, and then the firelight picked out the long barrel of a rifle, and as the three black men moved to surround them she felt the first taste of fear in her throat.

Steeves said with a gasp, "I say, who the hell—what *is* this?"

They had arrived so silently, their steps muted by the sound of the rapids, that Mrs. Pollifax found it difficult to believe in their reality. It was like opening one's door in July to find Halloweeners on the doorstep. Then Julian, looking grim, said, *"Nguti?"* and she knew these men were real and dangerous.

In excellent English the leader said, "If you move we shoot. We wish only hostages. You," he said, pointing to Mrs. Pollifax. "You—walk over here."

"Now wait a minute," said Cyrus, starting to rise from his chair, but one of the men reached out and pushed him down.

"And you," said their spokesman, pointing to Amy Lovecraft.

Mrs. Pollifax stood up, acutely aware of how snug the circle around the campfire looked. As she reluctantly crossed that circle, about to leave it, she became equally aware of each person she passed: of John Steeves looking furious, of Willem Kleiber shrinking back in his chair as if to make himself invisible, Lisa open-mouthed and plainly frightened, and Tom Henry studying the faces of the men with guns. When she reached the leader and turned, she saw that Cyrus was looking so outraged that she would have smiled if she hadn't felt so much like crying. It was, after all, dinnertime, and she was hungry and cold and she had the distinct feeling that she was not going to be fed.

And then Amy Lovecraft came up behind her and the leader said to his confederate, "Take them—quickly," and turning back he spoke across the fire to Julian. "You will remain very still, please. Your men on the hill have all been locked into the kitchen, your marconi is broken and your Land Rovers put out of action. I will have my gun on you, watching. I warn you, don't try to follow. Don't move."

"You're not Zambians," Julian said curtly, watching

him. "How did you get into the park?"

"That's our business."

Whatever else was said, Mrs. Pollifax was not destined to hear because she was being pulled away from the scene by one of the men. He gripped her tightly under one arm and dragged her in among the trees and along the river, then pulled her up a steep hill until she came face to face with a Land Rover waiting in the darkness. A rope was tied around her wrists, binding them together tightly behind her back, and then she was shoved into the rear of the car and a rifle held at her chest. The rifle was lowered for the arrival of Amy Lovecraft, who was pushed in beside Mrs. Pollifax, and then one of the men climbed into the driver's seat and started the engine, the Land Rover backed, turned and waited.

"This is terrifying," whispered Amy Lovecraft. "Isn't there something we can do?"

"With our wrists tied and a rifle pointed at us?" said Mrs. Pollifax dryly, and concentrated on catching her breath after the rush up the hill.

She heard footsteps, a muffled laugh, and the third man swung into the seat behind them. "Let's get out of here—fast," he said. "Turn on the headlights and move it, we can't keep Sikota waiting."

CHAPTER

9

It was astonishing, thought Mrs. Pollifax, how furious she could feel at Aristotle as they bumped along the road in the darkness. It seemed to her the height of injustice that because of him she had come to Africa and now she was being carried off into the night while he remained back at the campfire safe, warm, unidentified and—most outrageous of all—looking forward to his dinner. Certainly Carstairs could never have foreseen such an ironic ending to her mission. Her first reaction to being abducted struck her now as tiresomely pious: she'd actually thanked heaven that Chanda had been given a film so that if anything happened to her there would be a record left behind for Carstairs. Her reaction now was much less noble: she felt that she would resent very much anything happening to her, she *thoroughly* resented being lifted out of her safari, and under no circumstances did she feel that a few snapshots were an adequate exchange for a life. She was also hungry.

She turned and looked at Amy Lovecraft in the dim light from the dashboard and noticed that her hands were tied in front instead of behind her, and Mrs. Pollifax resented this very much too. In fact the depth of her indignation surprised her. Her own hands were tied in the back, which made it impossible to lean against the seat or to relax for even a second; it also demanded a great deal of effort from her just to remain on the seat, which was slippery. It was depressing, too, to reflect that of all the people on safari Amy Lovecraft was the last person she would have chosen as companion in such a situation. The woman was incalculable.

Having brought out her grievances and inspected them, Mrs. Pollifax began to feel better. About her abduction and her hunger she could do nothing, but she could at least try to like Mrs. Lovecraft. There had to be something lovable about her, she thought, and if they were going to be captives together she'd jolly well better find it now. She said in a comforting voice, "They'll come after us, you know, it will be all right."

Amy Lovecraft turned and looked at her. "After us?" she said, her lip curling. "Yes, but when exactly? And what the hell do you mean by 'all right'?"

Well, nothing lovable yet, thought Mrs. Pollifax, and decided to postpone any fresh attempt for the moment. Besides, she had discovered that by wedging herself sideways into the corner she could maintain a precarious balance, which was providential because the Land Rover suddenly turned off the road and plowed through the tall grass. They jolted ahead for several hundred feet and then came to a stop, went into reverse and backed out into the road again.

"I wonder what that was all about," said Mrs. Pollifax.

"I know a few words of Nyanga," said Mrs. Lovecraft, and leaned forward and spoke to the driver. She appeared to know quite a number of words, and the driver to speak Nyanga, because he replied at some length.

"He refuses to say," Mrs. Lovecraft told her, sinking back into her seat. "He doesn't want us to talk either."

"It was probably an attempt to confuse anyone following us," said Mrs. Pollifax sagely. "I hope that at some point he'll tell us why we're hostages."

Amy Lovecraft shrugged. "It's usually money, isn't it?" she said indifferently.

Mrs. Pollifax moved out of her corner and tried bracing herself with both feet against the floor. The road ahead was empty even of guinea fowl tonight, and she could see nothing on either side: there was only the dim light from the dashboard silhouetting the two men in front of her, and beyond this the bright twin beams of light combing the rough road. She and Amy Lovecraft huddled in the rear in darkness, with the third man crouched behind them; at times she could feel him breathing down her neck.

They were heading north, she knew, because they had made the same turn to the right after leaving camp that Julian had made this morning when he took them north to look for lions. She tried to recall her map of Kafue Park and, closing her eyes, remembered that it was shaped roughly like the state of Florida, that it was large and it was long, and that there were police posts at various intervals along its border. Only two roads entered it. The road that ran the length of the park from top to bottom, or south to north, was the road on which they were driving now, this narrow dirt road gutted with elephant holes which, for all its simplicity, remained the supply line that laced together the camps at Kafue Park.

The second road ran from east to west and was the paved Lusaka–Mumbwa highway by which they had entered the park on Monday, with its police stations at either end. Thinking about this, she decided that her abductors were either mad or uncannily shrewd, because they were heading precisely where they shouldn't go. They had Lufupa camp somewhere ahead of them—the camp at which they'd picnicked at noon—and Moshe camp above that, near the top of the park, while behind them they had Kafwala camp and the Lusaka–Mumbwa highway. This left them with only one large tract of land in which to maneuver, and she wondered how they proposed to get out of it. She also began to wonder why they'd chosen to snatch their tourists in a park since there must be tourists in far more accessible places . . . Lusaka for one, or Livingstone. It was all very illogical and baffling.

She opened her eyes to discover that the Land Rover was leaving the road again and stopping. This time one of the men climbed out and walked back through the tall grass, and during the interval he was gone the driver had time to light a cigarette and smoke it. When the man returned, the driver snuffed out his cigarette and started the engine, but this time he didn't slip the gear into reverse, he drove ahead into the bush, leaving the road behind. With this act something unalterably changed. It had been a modest road, thought Mrs. Pollifax wistfully, but it was a road that led back to Kafwala camp or ahead to Lufupa, or even indirectly to the city of Lusaka. Leaving it was like cutting an umbilical cord.

The ground was smoother now, but they drove fast and there were small hills and hollows to unsettle Mrs. Pollifax, so that at one point she ended up on the floor. Somewhere off in the distance a hyena howled, and Mrs. Pollifax longed to join with it and howl too. They drove on and on, it seemed interminable, the men occasionally exchanging sharp grunts or pointing up to the stars. It was a long time before they bumped to a halt, and before the headlights were extinguished Mrs. Pollifax glimpsed the shapes of two abandoned, crumbling huts inside a circle of trees.

The man sitting behind her said sharply, "Set up the radio, Reuben, we're ten minutes late."

"But Simon—"

"Later. Set up the radio—anywhere—but fast."

From one of the huts the two men carried out a heavy dark object, set it down on the grass and leaned over it. A candle was lighted, Simon squatted down in front of it, slid up an antenna and began fiddling with dials. His voice when he spoke was quite clear in the still night. Mrs. Pollifax heard, "Simon to Green-Bird, Simon to Green-Bird . . ."

Simon to Green-Bird suddenly broke off. "Got him," Simon said triumphantly, and then, "All okay here, Green-Bird, couldn't be better. What about your end?" He chuckled, listening. "Perfect. We follow through then as planned? My watch says 9:05 . . . Right. Twenty-one hours from now at Location B. Last contact, Green-bird. Signing off."

He slid the antenna back and nodded with satisfaction. "Smooth as silk, Mainza. You and Reuben take the candle and hide the radio." He paused, glancing around him. "I'll take the hut on the right. Reuben, you guard its door."

Turning back toward the Land Rover, his voice exhilarated, he said, "Out, ladies. Climb out and follow me."

They were led inside, and when a lantern had been lighted its illumination proved beyond any doubt that the men had been here earlier, for besides the radio that had been magically produced, there were sleeping bags in the corner, two boxes and a tarpaulin. The hut was small, perhaps eight feet square, and only three of its walls remained standing. Simon unfurled the tarpaulin and hung it over the fourth wall, which had crumbled away leaving only the wooden framework.

"Who are you?" asked Mrs. Pollifax as the lantern shone on Simon's face.

"It's of no importance," he told her.

"But you're not Zambians?"

He laughed. "No, not Zambians." Unrolling a sleeping bag he tossed it to Amy Lovecraft. "You—over there. Sit quietly, I wish to question this lady."

Amy Lovecraft carried the sleeping bag to the corner and sat down, her back against the wall, her bound wrists held out in front of her. She had been silent for a long time, and she remained silent, her eyes watching Simon intently. Perhaps she was weighing the possibilities of using feminine wiles on him, thought Mrs. Pollifax, but this was pure conjecture: at least she was subdued and not hysterical.

Simon carried one of the two boxes to the center of

the hut and gestured to her to sit down. She ignored this, saying stiffly, "My wrists hurt. You tied Mrs. Lovecraft's wrists in front of her and I don't see why mine can't be tied that way too."

Simon shot a quick glance at Amy Lovecraft and shrugged. He called, "Reuben?"

"Yes, Simon."

"Come in and guard this woman while I change the ropes on her wrists."

So much for that, thought Mrs. Pollifax, thinking wistfully of a back strangle, a front choke or a forearm slash; nevertheless, she was grateful to have her arms no longer pinned tightly behind her, and the relief to her shoulder muscles was exquisite.

"Now," said Simon. He produced the other wooden box and sat down opposite her, so close that their knees touched.

"Yes, now," said Mrs. Pollifax dryly. "What is it you want of us? What kind of ransom are you asking, and why?"

He brushed this aside indifferently. "The ransom requirements have already been delivered to the television station in Lusaka, madam. They became known at the precise moment we removed you from Kafwala camp. Now all you need do is co-operate. We wish information from you, it is a matter of photographs."

"Photographs," echoed Mrs. Pollifax, suddenly alarmed.

He did not notice her reaction, which was merciful, because a second later he was sliding four glossy six-by-ten-inch photographs from a crisp manila envelope, and Mrs. Pollifax could see at once that they were not hers.

"These," he said, and placing his gun on the floor he

handed her the pictures. "You will tell me which of these men is familiar to you."

"Familiar?" she said blankly. "But you must know I can't help you, I arrived in Zambia only Monday. It's ridiculous to think I could identify—"

"You will look at the photographs," he said flatly. "They are large and quite clear. We wish your impressions."

As she picked them up he leaned closer, his eyes on her face, and she thought, *Be careful, something is important here.* Because of this, instead of rifling through them quickly she kept them one on top of the other and approached them warily. The first was a color photograph of a long-faced man with a sweeping handlebar mustache and curly gray hair. Nothing there. The second was of another mustached man, very swashbuckling, with a bold look. She eyed him politely and then turned to the third picture, which was of—of John Sebastian Farrell, she realized in astonishment—*Farrell!*—and with a desperate concentration she forced herself to look into his face without expression before she wrenched her gaze to the last photo, a black-and-white picture of a plumpish hard-faced man.

She said, "They all have mustaches. I'm supposed to know one of them?"

"You *do* know one of them," he said, anger creeping into his cool voice. "You advertised for him in the *Times of Zambia.*"

She allowed her surprise to show; it was genuine but not for the reason he supposed. "I advertised for a man named John Sebastian Farrell," she told him. "Is *that* why you abducted me? You've just told us it was for ransom."

He shrugged. "The ransom scarcely matters. You know this Farrell, you can identify him for us, and that is what matters. The ransom is only—what do you call it, the red herring?"

This was rather staggering news. She gasped, "You amaze me," and then, accusingly, "Why was it necessary to kidnap two of us, then? Why Mrs. Lovecraft as well?"

"Two are always better than one," he said with a faint smile. "She will be hostage to *you*."

Over his shoulder Mrs. Pollifax glanced at Mrs. Love-craft to see how she was taking this news of her expendability, but she appeared to have withdrawn into a world of her own, her brows knit together, her eyes blank. In the dim light of the lantern she looked bloodless, her face the same shade as her pale hair. "I didn't realize Farrell was such an important person," she said, turning back to Simon. "Why?"

"That is *our* business. Which of these four is he?" He leaned forward, his eyes narrowed. "You understand we know one of these men is Mr. Farrell, we *know* this, so you will now tell us which he is."

"But none of them *is* Mr. Farrell," she lied.

He hit her hard across the face with the back of his hand, brutally, without emotion. "I don't think you understood the question."

She looked at him, blood running from her cut lip into her mouth, her anger matching his as their eyes met. She said steadily, "And you are not a very nice person."

"You see that? Good. Now look again at these pictures."

"No," she said, turning away, "because those men are strangers to me."

"Look at them," he shouted, and held the first one in front of her eyes, one hand encircling her neck and forcing her to look. "This one?"

"No," she gasped.

He held out the second. "This?"

She shook her head.

"This one, then?"

"I told you—none of them," she cried, her fury outweighing her terror.

He hit her again, this time so savagely that she fell off the box to the floor. Behind him Mrs. Pollifax heard Amy Lovecraft begin to cough, and impatiently Simon leaned over and pulled her to her feet.

"Listen to me," he said in a hard voice. "To me you are so much carrion. We do not leave this place until the sun rises tomorrow morning and there will be more of this, much more. I will drag this information from you the hard way or the easy way, but *you will give me what I want*. Think about this, it is your choice."

He stalked out.

There was a long silence, and then in the corner of the hut Mrs. Lovecraft stirred and sighed, her trance ended. She lifted her head and looked at Mrs. Pollifax and she said, "You were absolutely super, you know. I hope I wouldn't have told them what they want, either."

Licking the blood from her broken lip, Mrs. Pollifax said angrily, "It's ridiculous, I really believed we'd been kidnaped for money."

"Yes, but what will you do when this Simon comes back?" she asked, looking at her curiously. "How long do you think you'll be able to trick him?"

Mrs. Pollifax had been wondering why Simon chose such a strange moment to break off his interrogation when a few more blows might have broken her; it was odd, she thought, his giving her this time to convalesce. Now she reluctantly turned her attention to Amy Lovecraft. "Trick him?" she said. If Amy believed that she could identify Farrell then this was a notion that had better be dispelled at once. Mrs. Lovecraft was speaking in a low voice but one of the walls was of canvas, and Simon—yes, Simon had definitely chosen a very curious moment to leave. "Trick him, Mrs. Lovecraft?"

"Oh call me Amy," she said impatiently. "Of course you were tricking him, it's what I would have done too, but you can't keep it up forever. The man is frightening. What are we to do?"

"There's nothing we can do," she said, and sat down and faced her. "None of those men was Mr. Farrell."

"Simon seemed certain of it."

"That's his problem."

"But you must see that we're in this terrible mess together," cried Amy. "It's so unfair. You have something to bargain with, but I—" She lifted her bound hands helplessly, her voice trembling. "I've nothing. I have to depend entirely on you because of this mysterious man they called Farrell. Who is he anyway? And how do you happen to know a man who lives in Zambia?"

"If he *does* live here," pointed out Mrs. Pollifax, and hoping that Simon was listening behind the tarpaulin she said in a clear voice, "Actually he's a man who lived next door to us years ago in New Brunswick, New Jersey. That's in the United States," she added parenthetically.

"A very delightful young man except of course he can't be young now, for it must be twenty or twenty-five years since I've seen him. I'll tell you how nice a person he is," she confided. "He helped my son build a soapbox car when he was twelve years old. He was devoted to Roger."

She saw that Mrs. Lovecraft—Amy—was regarding her with astonishment and she began to expand on this further, developing a touching story of boyhood escapades, of families moving and losing touch, and then, "It was Mr. McGillicuddy," she said, beginning to enjoy herself. "I ran into him on the street in New Brunswick several weeks ago. He'd known the Farrells very well, and he was amazed to learn I was going to Zambia on safari. He said John Sebastian was living here; he knew because they still exchange Christmas cards, and for the past few years he'd sent his in care of Barclay's Bank."

Amy's mouth, which had dropped open, closed with a snap. "And because of this you advertised for him in a newspaper? How could you be such a fool? How could you do such a thing? Just see what it's led to!"

"Well, I certainly didn't expect it to lead to this," pointed out Mrs. Pollifax reasonably. "But what Simon doesn't understand," she added, "is how very difficult it is to identify a man one hasn't seen for years. Perhaps I'd recognize him if he walked into this hut, but from a photograph, after twenty-some years?" She hesitated and then added warmly, "He used to call me the Duchess, you know—quite teasingly, of course—but he was that sort of child, very affectionate with adults, and so aware. Such a nice boy," she concluded, and her nostalgic smile was genuine enough: she was hearing Farrell roar with laughter at her story.

Amy appeared unmoved. She said, "I don't know why you can't trust me. I think you're telling me a lot of nonsense. You were very brave with that terrible man Simon but you're not talking to Simon now. I think you're playing games with me."

Mrs. Pollifax began to wish that Amy were a little more perceptive so that she would understand the situation. She said, "My lip is bleeding and my jaw hurts and I don't feel very much like games, I can assure you."

"But you must know one of those men," said Amy, "and I mind very much your not being frank with me. My God, it's my life too, you know. We ought to talk— make plans—because once you identify this man they'll let us go free, they'll return us to the safari, we'll be out of this nightmare."

Mrs. Pollifax doubted this very much but she thought that to say this would imply a working knowledge of evil that had best be concealed for the moment; it seemed far more sensible to maintain the façade of a woman who had never met with anything more violent than a snub from her garden club president over the identification of a knotweed. She felt it rather naïve of Amy to believe that Simon would return them to the safari if she identified Farrell. He had said the ransom was only a red herring; how would he explain this if she and Amy were returned to camp? It was more likely that he would simply abandon them in the bush and let them fend for themselves, and even this, she thought, was the happiest alternative; she could think of others far worse. She had not, for herself, detected any signs of altruism in the man. She said crossly, "That's all very well but I can't tell them what I don't know."

She stood up and began to walk restlessly around the
hut, Amy's eyes following her, and then she moved to
the corner and pushed aside the tarpaulin with her bound
hands and looked outside.

The first thing she discovered in the moment before
the guard saw her was that Simon was not, after all, glued
to the canvas listening to their conversation. She could
see this clearly because two lanterns hung suspended from
the branch of a tree, creating a circle of light in which
Simon and Mainza were siphoning gasoline from a drum
into the tank of the Land Rover. Above the lanterns a
tarpaulin had been clumsily rigged to conceal the light
from above, suggesting that it was search planes that
worried them.

But it literally staggered Mrs. Pollifax to realize that
Simon had not been eavesdropping on them. When the
guard turned and lifted his rifle threateningly she dropped
the edge of the tarpaulin and returned to her orange
crate, but she remained shaken by this discovery. Why
hadn't Simon been listening? He struck her as a very
clever young man, and she simply couldn't conceive of
his missing such an opportunity. He'd left behind him
two frightened women, alone together for the first moment since they'd been snatched from Kafwala camp. He'd
made his demands and then he'd hit her and then he'd
walked out, leaving behind him the perfect climate for
confessional. He must have known that something would
have to be said about Farrell, but he'd not even troubled
to listen. He was either very sure that he had all the time
in the world to extract information from her, or he was
not so clever as she'd thought him, or—

"I'm going to get some sleep," she said abruptly. "Simon said we'd be here until dawn, didn't he?"

"Sleep!" cried Mrs. Lovecraft.

"Yes, sleep. I'm really very tired, and not as young as you are," she pointed out, tugging at a sleeping bag. She pressed it flat with her bound hands, sat down and inserted herself into it. "If you wouldn't mind extinguishing that lantern—"

"I *would* mind," snapped Mrs. Lovecraft.

Mrs. Pollifax only nodded and turned her face to the wall away from the light. She stretched one leg and then the other; the ground was very hard and her bones sharp, but she had no intention of sleeping. Outside she could hear one or two murmurs from the men, and somewhere very far away the haunting cry of an animal. She attempted a gentle snore, moved and then settled down to the business of pretending sleep, surprised at how difficult it was.

What she wanted to think about in particular—and think hard—was the sobering fact that she had not, after all, been selected for this abduction at random. This needed growing used to, it changed every premise and, above all, her prospects. The kidnaping had been arranged exclusively for her, and because it was due entirely to her advertisement in the *Times of Zambia* on Tuesday morning it must also have been arranged very hastily. But this in turn led her thoughts to Farrell, and to the most pressing question of all: who was Farrell now, and what had he become that he was the object of a policeman's inquiry and the motivation behind this insane abduction?

She tried bringing back into her mind the photograph of him she'd just been shown, but all she could remember

of it was her response, the shock like a whiplash that had
hit her. It had not been the clearest of pictures, she recalled, but she'd recognized him at once, for what was
recognition, after all? Certainly it was not the shape of a
nose or mouth or jaw but a matter of essence and of
memory that stemmed from an organ far different from
the eye. It was instant and it was inexplicable. And now,
whatever he was up to, she was going to have to protect
him for as long as she could, while she waited for de-
liverance or an opportunity to escape. It was not a
pleasant thought.

She had been feigning sleep for perhaps fifteen minutes when she heard the sound she'd been waiting for.
Amy Lovecraft rose from her sleeping bag, blew out the
lantern and stood quietly in the middle of the hut, listening, and then she moved noiselessly to Mrs. Pollifax's
side and leaned over her. Hearing no change in her
breathing, Mrs. Lovecraft tiptoed across the hut, lifted
the tarpaulin and walked outside.

There was no outcry.

"She's asleep," Mrs. Lovecraft told the guard in a low
voice, and then, "Where's Simon?"

Mrs. Pollifax pushed back her sleeping bag and sat up.

"She's asleep," she heard Amy repeat.

"She's talked? She's told you everything?"

It was Simon speaking, but in so low a voice that Mrs.
Pollifax left her sleeping bag and crept across the earth
floor to place her ear against the tarpaulin.

". . . some improbable story I don't believe for a
minute. How long do we have before we kill her?"

"Until Sikota comes. We meet him at nightfall across
the Lusaka–Mumbwa road at an old burial ground. I

have compass instructions. That gives us twenty hours and we'll need them if they begin a search. But she could be useful, *Tsa*, like tethering the goat to capture the lion."

Mrs. Lovecraft said impatiently, "We can't linger, you know that. By Saturday I've got to be far away, and so must you. We can't take her with us, she has to be disposed of inside of twenty hours whether she talks or not. I thought by now—"

"This was your idea, *Tsa*."

"Don't be impertinent," she snapped. "If you do your work well she'll talk, I promise you. She's a fool, but she could be a clever fool. Hit her harder, Simon, and then I suggest . . ."

Their voices receded as they walked away and Mrs. Pollifax crept back to her sleeping bag and sat in it shivering. *If you do your work well she'll talk, I promise you* . . . the words hung still in the air. It was not pleasant to realize that her wildest guess had turned into fact: there had been no need for Simon to eavesdrop because Amy Lovecraft had never been a hostage at all, she was only pretending to be one in the hope that Mrs. Pollifax might confide to her what she refused to tell Simon.

She ought to have realized the complicity earlier, she thought, considering this, and perhaps a part of her had, for she had minded *very* much—with an astonishing anger —that Mrs. Lovecraft's wrists had been bound together in front of her, giving her so much more comfortable a ride. There had been a curious lack of alarm in her attitude too, and surely her exchange of words with the driver on the road had proven a lengthy one, considering the size of her query. There was Mrs. Lovecraft's persistence in not believing her about the photographs . . . her performance had been convincing but her skepticism had continued for perhaps a shade too long in a situation where they both were victims. More than this, though, there had been a growing awareness in her that Simon had known just whom to abduct at Kafwala camp, which implied that someone on the safari had been involved.

She remembered now the palms rustling at Chunga camp after her interview with Lieutenant Bwanausi, and Mrs. Lovecraft in the office as she passed. There was the radio message that Julian had mentioned her sending too. Not your typical tourist, thought Mrs. Pollifax angrily, a woman who traveled on safari and then casually called in cutthroats from Lusaka for an abduction. Her talents as an actress had been superb too; in retrospect there seemed a downright innocence about Amy's lusting after every man in the party.

But for how long could she hold out against torture, she wondered now, as she objectively examined a situation that was more hopeless than she'd realized. Simon had announced that they would stay in this hut until dawn, and soon he would come back primed by Amy to hit her harder, and with whatever fresh suggestions Amy had made after they passed beyond hearing. Twenty hours lay ahead of travel, alternated with torture, and at the end of them she was to be killed.

And no one but herself would ever know why. As a bona fide hostage there had always been hope, because many hostages survived, but she saw now that it was going to be Mrs. Lovecraft who survived this particular ordeal. She could even guess at a scenario: after she had been killed tomorrow night there would be Sikota to smuggle Simon, Reuben and Mainza out of the park by some clever means, and then, following a suitable length of time, Amy Lovecraft would stumble out of the bush in a state of hysteria. There would be a few artful scratches and buises, a terrifying tale of how Mrs. Pollifax had been murdered while attempting to escape. And who would not believe her? Amy would be a heroine.

And for so long as these wrists of hers remained bound, thought Mrs. Pollifax, that scenario was going to proceed very smoothly toward her murder and Amy Lovecraft's elevation to sainthood. She minded this very much, but even more, she realized, she mourned the comfortable illusion that she'd just lost of having a confederate of her own here, however unstable. Until a moment ago she'd believed they were three men against two women. Now there were suddenly four people against one—and she was the one—and it felt lonely.

The tarpaulin opened—Mrs. Pollifax could see the dark sky and the stars beyond it—and Mrs. Lovecraft tiptoed back to her sleeping bag. She had just settled into it when someone outside gave a startled cry.

Simon called, "Ssh—no, leave the lights. Reuben?"

"Here, Simon."

"Be silent. Wait."

The shout did it; Mrs. Pollifax rose from her sleeping bag and went to the tarpaulin, leaving Amy to her own dissembling, which consisted of sharp gasps and, "What's that? What woke me?" Ignoring her Mrs. Pollifax pulled back the flap and looked out. The lanterns were still lighted under the tree, but Simon and Mainza stood rigid now, both staring out into the bush. Following their gaze Mrs. Pollifax saw a large shape moving through the grass

toward the camp, too tall to be a lion, too slender to be
an elephant. The apparition moved steadily and noisily
toward them, a bulky, man-shaped silhouette against the
night sky, and then as it drew closer the farthest projec-
tion of the light picked out a pair of ragged sneakers,
then a pair of bluejeans followed by a sweater and
jacket until it reached the face of Cyrus Reed.

She had to be dreaming, thought Mrs. Pollifax.

He came to a stop and stood there, looking big and
wondrously normal and not at all ruffled. "Hello," he
said amiably, blinking at the sudden brightness. "Saw
your lights. Damn tiresome wandering about out there
in the bush. Mrs. Pollifax around somewhere, and Mrs.
Lovecraft?"

CHAPTER
10

Standing just behind Mrs. Pollifax, Amy said furiously, "Oh, the *fool!*" and then she recovered herself and added with less heat, "Now he's a hostage too!"

"Yes," said Mrs. Pollifax dazedly, "but how do you suppose he ever found us?"

Reuben turned and saw them and waved his rifle menacingly. Mrs. Pollifax dropped the tarpaulin and retreated to her orange crate and sat down to wait, her heart beating very fast, her thoughts in a turmoil. Several minutes later the tarpaulin lifted and Cyrus stepped inside the hut with his wrists tied together. He stood in the improvised doorway, blocking it completely, and Mrs. Pollifax thought that she'd never been so glad to see anyone before in her life. His glance took in Amy Lovecraft, lingered a moment without expression on Mrs. Pollifax's torn lip, and then he said in his mild voice, "Damn good to see you."

"Oh Cyrus," she said simply, "how on earth did you get here?"

"More to the point," interjected Amy sharply, "did you come alone?"

"Sorry about that," he told her. "No U. S. Cavalry racing to the rescue but there should be soon. Chanda's gone to get help."

"Chanda?" said Mrs. Lovecraft incredulously.

Cyrus nodded, looking pleased. "Damn clever boy, Chanda, or *ba na mâno*, as he puts it in Bemba. Damn clever at tracking too. We were only half an hour behind you. Slowed us down a bit, that false turn off the road you made, but it took Chanda only a few minutes to look over the signs and guess the trick. Learning a lot on this safari," he said, smiling at Mrs. Pollifax.

"But tell us how you got here," cried Amy, looking as if she wanted to shake him. "You can't have walked, and the Land Rovers—they said the Land Rovers—"

She had almost given herself away there, thought Mrs. Pollifax, watching her.

"Oh, yes, all the tires were slashed," Cyrus told her cheerfully, "but these ruffians who carried you off didn't realize there were spares in the storage hut. Julian took off in a great hurry for Chunga in one of the cars. Wanted to radio the police, he said . . . organize search parties. Seemed a damn shame nobody thought of following you while the trail was hot. *I* thought of it, and Chanda thought of it, so we had a little talk and stole a Land Rover."

"Just like that," said Amy with a hollow laugh. "How

—how original! Then you've brought a Land Rover here?"

"Not exactly here," he conceded. "Got mired in a swamp piece of land half a mile away. Thought we'd have to sit there until dawn, the two of us, but then we saw the light here. Chanda gave me escort—just to be sure I didn't tangle with any lions—and then took off into the night for Kafwala."

"On foot?"

"On foot," nodded Cyrus, giving her a curious glance. "Something wrong?"

"No, not at all, but what a story," said Mrs. Lovecraft. "Then Chanda will be coming back with help very soon?"

Mrs. Polifax wanted to cry out, *Don't say any more,* but she sat helpless and irresolute, not wanting Amy to learn that her connivance was known.

"Afraid not soon," confessed Cyrus. "Not *that* many spare tires. Julian's got four on his Land Rover but he's down at Chunga camp now. Other four are on the Land Rover stuck out there in the bush. Only a matter of hours, though."

"How—how comforting," said Mrs. Lovecraft, attempting another brittle laugh.

If Amy was laughing, Mrs. Pollifax was struggling against tears. Her emotions had never felt so battered; at sight of Cyrus her spirits had gone skyward, but now they were plummeting as she realized with a sense of horror what his arrival meant for him. She was touched by his courage, appalled by his recklessness and comforted by his reliable and enormous presence. At the same time—just to complicate the tangle—she wanted to laugh at the comic note he was introducing into the situa-

tion. For instance, he was blocking Simon's entrance into
the hut now, which became more and more obvious from
the rude noises outside. Cyrus turned, looked down, said,
"Oh—sorry," and Simon emerged from behind him
looking very much like an angry puppy riding herd on a
Saint Bernard.

Simon said sharply to Mrs. Lovecraft, "Out—quickly.
I separate you now. Into the other hut."

Mrs. Pollifax had wondered how they would confer
about this development, and she thought that Simon
managed it very convincingly; in turn, Amy Lovecraft
managed to look convincingly frightened as she walked
out ahead of him. As soon as the tarpaulin fell in place
behind them Mrs. Polifax whispered, "Be careful what
you say, he's really taking Mrs. Lovecraft out to confer
with her."

"Confer?" said Cyrus, staring at her in astonishment.

She nodded. "When Amy thought I was asleep she
walked out and began talking to them about me. It turns
out that she's in charge of the whole thing, except for
someone called Sikota in Lusaka."

"Good God," said Cyrus, looking appalled. "And I was
about to ask if we ought to worry about her being taken
off alone like that. Glad you told me. Damn glad I came."

"Yes, because if Chanda hurries—how long do you
think it will take him to reach Kafwala on foot?"

Cyrus shook his head. "Too long," he said uneasily.
"And they'll know it. Shouldn't have told Amy about
Chanda."

"But how could you have not told her when you
thought she was a hostage too?" protested Mrs. Pollifax.
"And they would have insisted on knowing how you

found us, Cyrus. If you'd refused to tell them they would have followed your tracks to the Land Rover."

"Shouldn't have mentioned there being so few spare tires, either," Cyrus said gruffly. "Very bad. Who's this Sikota chap you mentioned?"

"He must be the man who delivered a ransom note to the television station in Lusaka at the same time we were captured. They talked to him by radio," she explained.

"Oh?" said Cyrus, digesting this. "Pity Julian couldn't have known that before he went dashing off to get the news out. Done better, I'm thinking, to have followed you."

"As you did," she said, smiling.

"Yes." He gave her a thoughtful glance. "Suppose you realize these are the same three men we saw at Lufupa camp this noon. Which of them hit you?"

"It doesn't matter, Cyrus."

"Try hitting you again," he said sternly, "and they'll have me to deal with."

She said unsteadily, "You should never, *never* have come after us like this, Cyrus. It was madness."

"Only thing I could think of to impress you, my dear."

"Impress me!"

"Well," he said with a boyish grin, "couldn't believe you'd give me a thought, coping with this bunch of hoodlums. Rather hard to overlook if I'm here. Too big."

She began to laugh, which tore open her cracked lip again and sent a stab of pain across her cheekbone, but it was amazing how much better she felt for it, and almost light-hearted. It fortified her for Simon's reappearance.

He walked in and gave Cyrus a nasty glance. "We do

not wait for dawn to leave," he said coldly. "Because of you we go now."

"Afraid of that," sighed Cyrus. "Sorry, my dear."

"It's all right," she said, but of course it wasn't. For just a few brief moments there had been a flicker of hope that Chanda might be able to bring rescue before dawn. And really it was so unfair, she thought helplessly, to see all of her plans to uncover Aristotle aborted like this. By now, back at camp, who knew what arrangements were being made to assassinate some unknown and unknowing victim?

"Mainza—" Simon's voice brought her back to the present, and she realized that her worries over Aristotle were a luxury just now. She had to resist distractions; her life and Cyrus' life depended upon it.

"Mainza, remove all but this lantern."

Mainza nodded and began rolling up the sleeping bags. "And while the car is being packed, we begin again," Simon told her, looking grim. "Sit, please, and you—" He pointed at Cyrus. "You will stand in the corner over there where I can observe you."

"Think not," said Reed mildly. "Bigger than you are. Don't plan to budge an inch."

Simon gave him a long, measuring stare. "You prefer that we shoot you instead?"

Cyrus shrugged. "No need to, you know. Only came to keep the ladies company. I'll stand where I am and watch—like a UN observer," he added helpfully.

Perhaps it was Cyrus' size or his mildness or a lingering sense of authority from his years on the bench, but it became obvious now to Mrs. Pollifax that Simon didn't know how to handle him. Cyrus was large, he was amiable and he exuded kindness, but he had an air about him of being immovable. Simon eyed him with resentment and then apparently decided to ignore him because he turned away and gestured Mrs. Pollifax to sit down.

"As I started to say, we begin again." He was forced to step back as Mainza passed him, his arms filled with sleeping bags. When Mainza had gone he sat down on the other box. "Now you will tell me *exactly* how you met this Mr. Farrell."

"Farrell?" said Cyrus, lifting an eyebrow in surprise. "So that's it!"

"Yes, Farrell," Mrs. Pollifax said, nodding, and then, "all right," and began her story again. She explained about the house in New Brunswick, New Jersey, her son Roger and the soapbox car, but this time she embellished the story with small artistic details. She added a soapbox derby in which Roger won a first prize of five dollars, and she gave Farrell a mother who played the piano and a father who owned a department store. "And then the father died," she added, tiring of the story. "That's when they moved away."

Mainza tiptoed in again and then went out with the remaining sleeping bags and a lantern. Simon did not comment on her story. He drew out the four photographs again and held up the lantern for her to examine them by. "Which?" he demanded, handing them to her. "Perhaps it will improve your memory if I tell you that your life depends on it."

Mrs. Pollifax examined them one by one, frowning appropriately while Simon studied her face. She noticed that numbers had suddenly appeared in pencil on the bottom corner of each photograph; Mrs. Lovecraft's idea, no doubt. "I don't recognize any of these men," she said again with finality.

"Mind if I look?" asked Cyrus, and when Simon only shrugged he took the pictures, glanced through them and shook his head. "Absolutely impossible," he said flatly. "None of these men could have lived next door to Mrs. Pollifax."

"I may ask why?" Simon's voice was biting.

"Look at her, look at them. Tough-looking chaps. You think she'd know such a person? None of them," he added with authority, "built a soapbox car in his life."

Smiling at him, Mrs. Pollifax thought, *You dear man, there are so many things you don't know about my friends, but you've become one. Solidly.*

Simon leaned closer to her. "I do not believe you understand me. If you remain stubborn we kill you— like that," he told her, snapping his fingers. "We kill this man too."

"Stay as stubborn as she pleases," said Cyrus. "Why this passion for having Mr. Farrell identified?"

"So we will know which of these four men he is," he said, exasperated. "Ah—Mainza, the Land Rover is ready?"

"Everything is inside, Simon."

"Then we go. Take them out, Mainza, I'll bring the lantern and tarpaulin. As for you," he told Mrs. Pollifax, "we talk again, but if you do not talk for me, Sikota is the man with a genius. For him *everyone* talks."

They climbed into the Land Rover. Apparently Amy's role of innocent hostage was to be continued because she was led out of the second hut by Reuben, her wrists still bound, and inserted between Mrs. Pollifax and Cyrus on the rear seat. A rope was threaded through each of their bound wrists and secured to either side of the car, giving them a primitive check against falling; evidently some rugged driving lay ahead.

Amy spoke only once. She turned her flawless profile to Cyrus and said coolly, "It was terribly sweet of you to come, Cyrus, but I hope you'll realize what you've done. Now we're both hostages to Mrs. Pollifax. They'll kill us first to persuade her to talk, and believe it or not this woman seems very willing to sacrifice us. She doesn't give a damn at all."

"Ha," was Cyrus' only response.

The Land Rover started with a jolt, and following this, in proportion to the distance they covered, all sense of time diminished for Mrs. Pollifax. It was not that the Land Rover drove so fast but that a relentless speed of fifteen miles per hour over rough ground abused every bone in the body. The headlights had been taped so that only the immediate ground could be seen, and frequently the Land Rover swerved to avoid a rock, and once a startled wild beast. At some point during the first hour— she supposed it was an hour—Cyrus observed that they were heading west, and then after an interminable length of time he announced that they seemed to be veering south, but except for these comments no one spoke. Mrs. Lovecraft remained silent and Mrs. Pollifax reflected that if Kafue Park was half the size of Switzerland, this gave Simon a great deal of space in which to maneuver, and any search parties vast difficulties in finding them.

It was kinder not to think of Aristotle. She began to think instead of how far she could go in protecting Farrell's life from whatever dangers these people represented, and she thought the dangers must be considerable if they would go to such lengths as an abduction. But there was Cyrus' life too . . . He had wandered after her, heroic and innocent, and it was unthinkable that he might have to pay for it with his life. She felt responsible for him even if he would snort indignantly at such an idea. How could one choose? One could say that Farrell was the younger, with more years ahead of him to live, but balanced against this was the fact that Farrell had survived to his forty-some years by outwitting just such people as Simon, and how could she assume that he wouldn't survive her identifying him? And on that score there rose the doubts—oh God, the doubts, she cried silently, those niggling, poisonous doubts that were perfectly logical but which she would do well to face now, and with honesty. Chance had brought her and Farrell together once in a very rare intimacy, but there was no overlooking the fact that their values had been different even then, and that four years had intervened since she'd known him. He might be smuggling drugs, or involved in something equally abhorrent to her. She could vividly remember her shock at first meeting him—that hard-bitten face and those mocking eyes . . .

She discovered that she was smiling as she remembered those first reactions of a refugee from the New Brunswick, New Jersey, Garden Club. What a sheltered life she'd led before she met him, and how she must have amused him! It was preposterous to think he could change that much. He was a man who'd not broken under torture, and when he believed he was going to his death his first thoughts had been of her. No, she couldn't betray him, she simply couldn't . . .

She realized that she couldn't betray Farrell and that she absolutely couldn't sacrifice Cyrus. She was going to have to wait and trust to her instincts hour by hour, and in the end—if they weren't found in time by a search party—there might be no choice at all, or very little, because even if she identified Farrell it might not save Cyrus' life. She would simply have to wait, and in the meantime, just because it was night and she was cold and hungry, she mustn't lose hope. In fact, if she could just get these ropes off her wrists, the bush country of Zambia would ring with her shouts of *Ki-ya*.

"Growing light," said Cyrus, lifting his bound wrists and pointing toward the horizon. "Must be nearly four o'clock."

Mrs. Pollifax looked up and for the first time since her capture saw the world around her. The light that he'd pointed out was murky, no more than a subtle diminishing of darkness, but it was enough to define thorn trees and tall grass and the slope of the ground. She felt totally unequipped for this new day, but slowly and softly a warm golden light stole over the earth, dissipating pockets of mist in the hollows, and then abruptly the sun spilled over the horizon, huge and orange, and Mrs. Pollifax's spirits rose with it.

Simon and Mainza began chattering together in the front, and at length called in their own language to Reuben in the back. Mainza pointed to the left, they swerved in that direction, entered a copse of trees and came to a stop.

"We rest," said Simon, turning off the ignition.

They climbed stiffly out of the Land Rover and were led to a cleared area which, mercifully, received the warmth of the sun. Reuben brought them sleeping bags which they spread on the ground, after which bathroom privileges were extended to them and they took turns going off, with Reuben as guard.

Simon and Mainza remained beside the car. As soon as Amy had gone, leaving her alone with Cyrus, she looked at him and said firmly, "It's absolutely imperative that we get these ropes off our wrists."

"Logical, my dear, yes," he said, nodding, "but for the moment impossible."

"Then, failing that," she said earnestly, "there ought to be some way for us to capture Amy and use her as a shield or hostage."

"Thought had occurred to me," admitted Cyrus, "but not with any solution. Have to add I'm not very good at this sort of thing."

She smiled. "It may surprise you what you can accomplish if your life depends on it."

"Yes, but say, for instance, I approach our friend Amy from the rear," he said, "and fling my bound wrists over her head and hold her as a shield, what then?"

"Then I stand behind you——"

"Two of us hiding behind Amy?" He smiled faintly. "Bit of a stalemate, I'd say."

"Why? They wouldn't dare to shoot us," she protested. "If they did they'd hit Amy."

"Could stand facing each other for days, though," pointed out Cyrus. "Or they'd circle us. Three against two, and they've guns."

Mrs. Pollifax bit her lip. "You have a point there, unfortunately. Oh, if only there were some way to free our *hands!*"

"What then?" he asked, looking at her with amusement.

"Well, you see I'm rather good at karate."

This startled him but there was no overlooking his gleeful appreciation of this. "*Damned* astonishing woman," he said. "Enough to goad me into chewing off your ropes with my bare teeth."

"I wish you could," she said wistfully. "They plan to kill me when we reach the burial ground, you know."

"Burial ground? Nothing," protested Cyrus, "has been said about a burial ground."

"That's what I overheard . . . it's across the Mumbwa–Lusaka highway, which we'll have to cross at some point, apparently, and around darkness they meet Sikota there."

"So," mused Cyrus. "The longer it takes us to reach the burial ground—a macabre meeting place to say the least—the longer we have to exercise cunning, I take it?"

She nodded. "Why is Mainza climbing that tree now?"

He turned to look. "Could be lost. See better from a tree."

"But they have a compass and maps."

"Simon's been poring over both since we sat down," he told her. "Very heavy frown on his face."

"I think it would be lovely if we're lost," she said, watching a scarlet butterfly hover over Amy's sleeping bag, touch down and then twinkle away. "I'd like to see it happen to them, they deserve it."

"Not so sure *we* deserve it," he pointed out. "Very tiring sort of thing, being lost. Makes men like Simon irascible and insecure. Better sleep now, my dear, it may be your only opportunity."

She nodded and lay down, and thinking how pleasant

it was to be called *my dear*—and how fortifying Cyrus
was—she closed her eyes and then opened them to watch
Mainza climb down from his tree. Amy was returning
from the bush—she could hear the crackle of dried leaves
and the snap of twigs—with Reuben's heavier footsteps
behind her. The sun and the warmth of the sleeping bag
combined to soothe her aching muscles and help her
forget her hunger; she closed her eyes a second time, felt
tiredness wash over her in waves and then engulf her,
and she slept.

When she opened her eyes the clearing was empty of
voices and she saw that Cyrus' sleeping bag was unoccu-
pied. Without moving her body she turned her head and
saw Amy burrowed deeply in her sleeping bag with only
strands of pale hair in sight. Over near the Land Rover,
Simon and Mainza were stretched out asleep in the sun.
Reuben sat dozing with his back against a tree, the rifle
across his lap, his eyes closed, but of Cyrus there was no
sign until a sudden stealthy movement from the Land
Rover caught her eye. It was Cyrus, creeping around the
back of the vehicle on hands and knees. Mrs. Pollifax
glanced at the dozing Reuben and then at Cyrus, and
held her breath in horror.

CHAPTER

11

She had no idea what Cyrus had been doing behind the Land Rover but he was in plain view of Reuben: only Reuben's closed eyelids—a fragile barrier—lay between him and discovery, and Cyrus' stealth was proof that he was up to something. She dared not lift her head lest the movement wake Reuben, who was obviously supposed to be thoroughly awake and guarding them. She lay very still and held her breath. Cyrus was still on his hands and knees, but when he reached the side of the Land Rover he slowly rose to his feet, glanced once at Reuben and then tiptoed soundlessly toward her, testing the ground underfoot at each step. Only when he had dropped to his sleeping bag did she sit up, and as she did so Reuben gave a start, opened his eyes and instinctively reached for his rifle.

"Feeling better?" asked Cyrus without expression. "About four hours' sleep, I think."

"Much better," she said politely.

The others were stirring now too, sitting up, and stretching, yawning, their faces cleared of tension and hostility, so that for a moment they might have been a picnic party waking up from a nap out in the bush. Simon called out something to Reuben, who laughed and replied, and then Mainza and Simon both laughed, completely relaxed. Only when Simon's glance fell on the map and the compass did his frown return. He picked them up and tension was visible again on his face.

Amy Lovecraft sat up and pushed back tangled hair with her tied wrists. "Oh God, how I'd love a bath," she said.

But the only water they were to see this morning was brought to them by Reuben in a canvas bag. They took turns drinking from it, and then he opened his palm and revealed a handful of peanuts. "Ground nuts," he said, dividing them equally among them.

"So that's what they're called here," said Mrs. Pollifax. He had thoughtfully shelled them and she tried to chew each one carefully—there were only eight—because they were both last night's dinner and today's breakfast as well. In fact, if this was Thursday she remembered that it was time for another malaria tablet, but she supposed it was trivial to worry about malaria when she might not even survive the day. Perhaps it was also trivial to worry now about Aristotle . . . Cyrus was conspicuously silent; he looked tired, and she realized he'd probably not slept at all, and again she wondered what he'd been doing crouched behind the Land Rover. She turned her head and glanced at Amy, and not for the first time speculated about her motives in this insane abduction. She wondered if Amy could possibly be Aristotle. Women *were* assassins, and clever at disguise, but Aristotle—Aristotle, she felt, was different. Bishop had described him as a professional and a mercenary, with no ties to any particular country. She simply couldn't imagine him involving himself in an abduction, and then there was the fact that Amy knew these men, and Aristotle always acted alone.

Her thoughts were interrupted by Simon, who shouted, "Up!" and once again they were herded to the Land Rover and loosely roped in place. They set off in the warm morning light, and Mrs. Pollifax noticed they avoided open spaces now, which she thought showed more faith in a search party than she could muster at the moment. Shortly after leaving they skirted another clearing and surprised a herd of zebra standing motionless in the sun. The herd took flight at once, their stripes dancing and blurring as they swept across the plain in a cloud of graceful motion, and then as they reached the edge of the clearing the Land Rover swerved and they came to a stop.

"Flat tire," said Simon.

They climbed out and sat on the ground while Mainza jacked up the Land Rover and removed the tire. The spare was taken from its mounting on the hood and inserted on the rim, the jack was disengaged and the Land Rover lowered until it came to rest on the new tire, which slowly, comically, went flat too.

It was at this moment that Mrs. Pollifax sensibly added two and two together and glanced with interest at Cyrus. He was looking exceptionally sleepy and he refused to look at her. Deep inside of herself she smiled; really, she thought, Cyrus was going to be extremely useful now that he was getting into the swing of things. Simon, Reuben and Mainza were looking incredulous; they began talking accusingly among themselves, examining the two tires and gesticulating. She gathered that both tires had lost their valve caps but that the men found it difficult to undersand how this could have caused so much leakage of air. Several suspicious glances were sent in their direction, but since no one could recall a moment when they were unguarded no one accused them.

"Into the car," Simon said at last, his voice surly.

They climbed inside and bumped along on the naked rim of the wheel for several hundred feet until they hit a half-buried rock that bent the rim. The Land Rover at once acquired an unhealthy list that sent Amy and Mrs. Pollifax into Cyrus' lap, and the car out of control. With a shout of frustration Simon fought the Land Rover to a stop. "We walk," he said furiously.

"Sorry about this," whispered Cyrus as he helped her down from the Land Rover.

She gave him a frankly admiring glance. "You make a lovely fly in the ointment."

"You saw?" When she nodded he grinned. "Damn nuisance, walking, but makes me feel better. Vented my spleen, so to speak."

"Do vent it again," she shrugged over her shoulder as Simon commanded her to be silent and take her place in line.

They began their march with Simon in the lead. The terrain was a mix of flat ground and clusters of thorn trees, a combination not at all unpleasant for walking.

What Mrs. Pollifax minded was the silence in which they walked; a little conversation, she thought, would be a happy distraction, but Simon had placed her behind him and she was followed by Mainza; Amy and Cyrus came after him, and Reuben brought up the rear. It was so quiet that she could hear the swish of their trousered legs and the thud of Mainza's rifle as it slapped his hip at each step; occasionally twigs snapped underfoot. As the sun rose higher, however, she became increasingly aware of a hollowness in the pit of her stomach that only food could alleviate, and the sun, which felt no warmer to her skin than a June sun in New Jersey, began to have a curious effect on her; her head felt light, but whether this was from hunger or the sun she didn't know or, at the moment, care. She developed a nagging thirst, and after they had walked for an interminable length of time she suspected that she was also developing a blister on her right heel. The tse-tse flies gathered, and with her hands tied she could only swat at them blindly, but Simon showed no signs of halting for a rest and she found herself lacking even the energy to complain. It seemed simpler to plod dreamily along, her eyes mesmerized by the ground in front of her, her head floating along somewhere behind her, like a balloon on a string.

"Rest," said Simon suddenly, and they sank to the ground under a tree, too tired to speak.

Mainza brought out the canvas bag of water and gave them each a few sips.

"Boiled, I hope," said Cyrus.

Amy sniffed at this remark. "Even boiled water here can cause gastric trouble. If you'd only tell them what they want to know," she snapped at Mrs. Pollifax, turning to face her, "we could be back on safari with the others now, instead of—of *this!*"

Mrs. Pollifax, feeling better, snapped back. "Nonsense. I don't believe my telling them *anything* would free us now, because we can identify Simon and Mainza and Reuben, and why should they allow that?"

Amy moved closer and lowered her voice. "I've been trying to make friends with Simon, you may have noticed?"

"No," said Mrs. Pollifax.

"Well, I have, and I think—" She smiled disarmingly and a little ruefully, "I think they might not kill *me*. It's possible I could divert the three men so that you and Cyrus could get away. Not now but later."

Shot while trying to escape, thought Mrs. Pollifax. For just the briefest of moments she looked at Cyrus, who was listening to this, and then she turned to Amy and said in a shocked voice, "Oh, I don't think that would be sensible, do you? I suppose you mean an *escape*. I shouldn't care for that at all, would you, Cyrus?"

"No indeed," he said blandly. "Exhausting. Besides, our hands are tied."

"So are mine," said Amy, "but I might be able to persuade Simon to untie them."

I'll bet you could, thought Mrs. Pollifax. She said earnestly, "Well, it would certainly be lovely to have our hands free—it's so difficult walking with them tied—but as for escape—" She shuddered. "I don't know, the idea fills me with terror." She realized that Cyrus was looking at her with a puzzled frown and she wondered what she'd just said that made him suddenly look so suspicious of her. "But if you could persuade him to free our hands," she added wistfully.

"Yes," said Amy, "but you simply *must* consider getting away if the occasion arises. You have to be more resolute."

"Yes," sighed Mrs. Pollifax.

A moment later Simon announced that it was time to move on, and she learned the reason for Cyrus' peculiar expression. Helping her to her feet he said, "Beginning to wonder if you *do* show slides."

"Slides!" she gasped. "Cyrus, what on earth—!"

"Same voice," he said. "Both times. Been worrying about those slides."

She stared at him in astonishment. "Oh—*slides*," she said, realizing how alarmingly observant he was.

He added in a kind voice, "Try wrapping your bush jacket around your head. They didn't wear cork hats for nothing here in Africa. Very strong sun." He tugged loose the jacket that was knotted around her waist and she thanked him. Incapable of tying it around her head with her hands bound, she placed it there like a basket with trailing fronds and hurried off to obey Simon's peremptory summons.

They resumed walking, they stopped . . . they walked, they stopped. She was becoming very familiar with the African soil, she thought; it was a vivid rust color, with the coarse-grained texture of an anthill, and although the rainy season had only recently ended it was dry, very dry, providing only a vaguely hospitable surface to the stalks of grass. The earth was in fact kinder to her than to the vegetation, for she rested on it, and when Simon ordered them up again her only anticipation was to sit on it again. It was level enough for walking but it was important to watch out for snakes, and so she walked with her head down, which was tiresome. The tse-tse flies kept biting, and when they stopped for a break the meager sip of water doled out to them was no longer enough, and at each stop Simon examined both compass and map with the same frown teasing his brows. Then it was up again to resume walking, the monotony of it interrupted only twice—once by a herd of impala racing in panic across their path, and once by the sight of a dead buffalo lying on its side under a tree, with only the shell of its carcass untouched.

"Lion kill," said Reuben from the rear.

Sometime after that Mrs. Pollifax became aware that Simon had stopped. She had been stumbling along behind him when she looked up to see that Mainza had left his place in line and was grasping Simon by the arm, pointing behind them.

"Something is following us," Mainza said in a low voice.

"I see nothing. Animal or man?"

Mainza shook his head. "I don't know, it moves when we move, stops when we stop. If I go ahead to that hill, Simon, and circle back—"

"Do that. Be careful. We will rest behind the hill."

The word *rest* was all that mattered to Mrs. Pollifax and she followed Simon eagerly now. Mainza soon disappeared behind the swelling in the earth, and when they came abreast of it Simon led them around it and signaled them to stop. "Sit," he said, "but not on the hill, this is an anthill."

Mrs. Pollifax sank gratefully to the ground and applied

herself to resting with enormous concentration. Her shoulder bones, subtly hunched together by the pull of her tied wrists, were acquiring strange aches and pains; her feet hurt and her eyes felt like bruised grapes. This was having an effect on her thought processes that was alarming, and yet she felt incapable of any discipline at all; it was rather like watching oneself fall asleep in the snow and not caring. There would be no decent rest for her until they reached the burial ground, and she reminded herself that once they reached that destination her longed-for rest could very well become an Eternal Rest, but this reminder met with no response at all. It occurred to her to wonder if she was suffering from sunstroke. She saw Simon and Reuben level their rifles, suddenly tense, but she was only mildly interested when a man trudged unseeingly past them. She was grateful that he was not a lion, but the day held such a surrealistic quality that she found nothing surprising about their encountering a man here. Besides, he looked as if he belonged here and he was certainly not prepossessing. He was a native wearing torn black pants, cut off at the knee, a ragged pair of old sneakers on his feet and a brilliant plaid wool cap on his head that made him look ridiculous. A sweater had been rolled up and tied around his waist by the sleeves, and on his back he carried something wrapped in a bloody newspaper; it had weight to it, and there were a number of flies buzzing around it. The man noticed them only when Simon stepped forward with his rifle, but he looked startled rather than frightened. He gave Simon a radiant, uncertain smile and then his gaze dropped to the rifle and he gaped at it, fascinated. Apparently the rifle was more amazing to him than the sight of five people crouched behind an anthill.

Mainza came up from the rear and pointed his gun at the man, searched his pockets and sniffed at the bloody package.

"Jonesi," the young man said, beaming and pointing to himself. "Jonesi. Good evening."

"Good evening," however, turned out to be the only English that he knew. Mrs. Pollifax gathered that Nyanga was tried on him, as well as a few words of Luvale and Bemba, but these produced only excited nods from him and the words, "Jonesi. Good evening."

"Don't think he has all his wits about him," suggested Cyrus.

Mainza peeled back a corner of the bloody package and said accusingly, "He's been poaching, Simon. He's a poacher, his name is Jonesi, and what do we do with him?"

"I don't like him," Amy said suddenly in a cold flat voice.

Simon shot her a quick glance and without appearing to answer her said to Reuben, "He knows the land, he could help us find the burial ground."

"Ah," said Mrs. Pollifax, coming to life, "you don't know where the burial ground is?"

"Of course we know," snapped Simon, and then spoiled the effect by adding, "It's only that we've never traveled this way before."

"So you're lost?" said Amy sarcastically. "How thoughtful of you to tell us all about it, Simon."

"Don't see how this Jonesi's going to help if you can't even communicate with him," pointed out Cyrus.

But Mainza, having captured the poacher's attention, sat down cross-legged on the ground and began digging in the earth with a stick, forming a series of small mounds. When he had created half a dozen of these he placed a twig on one, a button on another, and a shred of cloth on a third. The poacher squatted beside him, watching doubtfully, until suddenly he nodded and burst out talking, pointing to the south and laughing. After more sign language Jonesi took the stick from Mainza and drew the rough outline of an animal, after which they made more sign language and Mainza stood up. "He knows the burial ground," he told Simon. "He'll take us there if we don't report his poaching. It's antelope meat in his sack."

Mrs. Pollifax thought about this carefully, aware of something there that she'd been too tired to catch. Antelope meat . . . She applied herself to this diligently: antelope meat, burial ground, poaching . . . but of course, she thought dizzily, Jonesi's meat was butchered meat, and if it had been butchered, then it had to have been cut from the carcass with a knife . . . a *knife.*

Her tiredness fell away from her like an old coat that had been ready for the Salvation Army anyway. Hope was all that she'd needed, and now it began flowing through her bloodstream like adrenalin. A knife. With a knife they could assert themselves and get away. A knife would free their hands for all kinds of gloriously hostile purposes.

"You look," said Cyrus as they rose to go, "like someone who's just found the Holy Grail."

She gave him a dazzling smile, and in the brief moment before Simon separated them she whispered, "Cyrus . . . the poacher has to be carrying a *knife.*"

CHAPTER

12

Mrs. Pollifax reasoned that her first efforts, now that she was aroused, ought to go into establishing some kind of relationship with the poacher. Under the circumstances she felt she could at least extend to him a small but heartfelt welcome, and then slowly hope to impress on him the fact that she and Cyrus were captives. If sign language had succeeded once with him, she could see no reason why it shouldn't succeed again.

She began to walk faster, accelerating her pace until she drew abreast of him. When he turned his head to look at her she smiled at him and won a huge and vacant grin in return. He was certainly the tallest Zambian she'd seen, probably six feet tall if he stood up straight, and so thin that his ribs could be counted under his flesh. His face was long and bony, and, combined with his protruding teeth, his senseless wide grin and that absurd green-and-black plaid wool cap, it gave him the look of a man definitely lacking in intelligence. Nevertheless he was not one of *them*, she had just deduced that he must be carrying a knife, and he was their only hope.

After they had exchanged a number of eager smiles, she felt that she had paved the way for a subtler message. When he turned again to look at her she lifted her tied wrists to his gaze. She did this discreetly. His eyes dropped to her hands, his smile broadened, and then he startled her by throwing back his head and laughing.

This was certainly depressing. The laugh drew a backward glance from Simon, and she had to pretend that she was lifting her wrists to push back her hair. She decided that making a bid for Jonesi's friendship at this point could be dangerous, and she fell back behind him in line.

This left her with her second challenge: where did a man who wore only sneakers, cap and shorts carry a knife? She guessed it would have to be in one of the pockets of his disreputable shorts until she remembered that Reuben had searched both of Jonesi's pockets and had seemed satisfied that he carried no weapons. If it wasn't in his trousers, she decided, then the knife would have to be concealed either in the rolled-up sweater around his waist or in his cap, and of the two she thought that she would vote for the cap: there was an elemental logic in this because the cap was obviously a prized possession, and the knife would be equally valued. She began to play with possibilities for getting the cap on his head and discovered that this happily removed all thoughts of hunger and thirst from her mind.

In midafternoon they came to the road. Simon signaled them to stop, and once they had straggled to a halt Mrs. Pollifax heard the unmistakable sound of a truck in the distance. It soon passed. Simon waited for them to form a circle around him, rather like a Boy Scout leader preparing to give instructions to his troop. "The road is just ahead," he explained. "We go two by two across it, and very quickly, you understand?" Pointing to Mrs. Pollifax he said, "You will go first, with Reuben and Mainza. Reuben, you will come back for the man, I will follow with the other woman. Listen before you cross, the wind blows from the west."

Mrs. Pollifax was led forward through a screen of trees until they came to the road, a two-lane macadam highway stretching from east to west. It was depressingly empty of traffic now. Reuben grasped one of her arms, and Mainza the other, and they hurried her across and into the shelter of trees on the opposite side. When Reuben went back for the others Mrs. Pollifax sat down, hoping it wasn't on an anthill, and tried not to think how near they must be to the burial ground now. *How long before we kill her? Until Sikota comes, we meet at the burial ground across the Lusaka–Mumbwa road.* It ran through her head like a macabre nursery jingle.

Seeing Reuben escort Cyrus to her through the trees, she thought now what an astonishing person Cyrus was and how comfortable he was just to look at, for nothing about him seemed changed. He might be tired but he remained completely unruffled, with the air of a solid man who knew exactly who and what he was even in the center of Zambia. It struck her suddenly that she would feel very lonely if she never saw him again.

"You look like a judge even here," she told him, smiling.

"Feeling very unjudgelike at the moment," he said, sitting down beside her. "I'd give each of these people six months in solitary. No bail, either. They walk too fast."

"I think," said Mrs. Pollifax in a rush of warmth, "that it's terribly selfish of me, but I'm awfully glad that you came, Cyrus. You *are* hard to overlook."

"Told you so," he said in a pleased voice.

"It was so—so very gallant," she explained. "Except that—if you should have to pay for it with—"

"No need to be tedious, my dear," he interrupted quietly. "Entirely my own choice, you know, didn't have to come. More to the point," he added lightly, "is the dinner I plan to buy you when we get back to Lusaka. Menu's been occupying me for hours."

She realized in a sudden spasm of perceptiveness that Cyrus was only too aware of how near they were to the burial ground. "I think it has to be in either his sweater or cap," she said in a lowered voice. "The knife, I mean —if he has a knife."

"Mmmm," murmured Cyrus. "Let's hope it gets cold then, and soon." He held up his wrists and scanned his watch. "Nearly four o'clock."

"Oh dear, and dark in two hours?"

"Must have walked about twenty miles. Saw a data bird, by the way. Pity I couldn't have pointed him out to you." He broke off as Simon strode toward them, apparently tireless, with Jonesi loping along beside him and Amy a pace behind.

"On your feet," said Simon, and that was the end of any further conversation.

It was perhaps ten minutes later that Jonesi called out sharply and pointed to the left, jabbering away in his language that no one understood. He appeared to know the terrain now because, once they veered off to the left, they encountered a narrow, hard-beaten path through the grass and soon came upon the ruins of several huts, their scaffolding lying in crazy patterns like jackstraws.

And then quite abruptly they reached the burial ground.

It lay in the sun at the edge of a broad savannah, and if Jonesi had not led them it was difficult to see how it could have been found. It was not large. Perhaps it marked the site of some ancient battle, or it was where chiefs or medicine men of this village were buried, for Mrs. Pollifax counted only twelve low mounds. There had once been the village, and people had lived here and guarded the graves, and then the villages had been moved when the land became a game park, but in the people's minds the burial ground still existed, still mattered, for the stakes at either end of each grave stood erect and undisturbed, and no one had touched the round earthenware pots that had been broken at death and lay scattered between the sticks. She liked that touch, thought Mrs. Pollifax, it seemed so much more personal than flowers. A pot would be something of one's own, used every day of one's life, and what better symbolism than to end its existence along with the life of the man who had carried it, drunk from it, cooked in it and eaten from it.

Cyrus interrupted her trancelike musings with a nudge. She turned and, following his gaze, saw that Jonesi had sat down and was removing the sweater from around his waist. She watched with Cyrus as the man carefully unrolled the sweater, picked a dried leaf from it, blew on it, smoothed it out and then pulled it over his head and shoulders. There was no knife, which left only his cap as a possibility.

"We wait for Sikota now, he will come within the hour," Simon said, and turning to Mrs. Pollifax, with a triumphant note in his voice, "No one has ever held out against Sikota. He knows many tricks, I promise you." The menace of this unpleasant statement was only slightly undermined when he added, "You are now extended bathroom privileges."

"Please," said Amy, and jumped to her feet and followed Simon in among the trees.

When the two of them were out of sight, Mrs. Pollifax looked down at Jonesi, seated cross-legged on the ground, and then at Cyrus, sitting with his back to the tree. Not far away Mainza and Reuben sat talking earnestly together, their rifles beside them. She thought, *It's now or never for the cap*, and meeting Cyrus' glance she said aloud, "It's now or never."

"Oh?" he said, puzzled.

She walked around Jonesi, and when she was behind him she pretended to stumble. She thrust forward her bound wrists, fell against him and shoved his cap from his head. It dropped to the ground in front of him, and just as she recovered her balance a second object fell with it, making a solid *plunk* as it met the earth.

It was his jackknife, stained with blood.

Both Jonesi and Cyrus reached for the knife at the same time. "Hope you don't mind," Cyrus said courteously, picking it up with one hand, and with the other handing Jonesi his cap. "There's a little matter of ropes, if you'll bear with us for a moment. Emily?"

She sat down next to the poacher and held out her wrists to Cyrus. With his hands bound together it was slow work—"like sawing through a redwood tree with a handsaw," he said grimly—but presently her bonds fell from her wrists and for the first time in twenty-four hours her hands were free. She flexed them with a sense of wonder and then took the knife from Cyrus and went to work.

"Of course they're going to notice our hands when they come out of the woods," murmured Mrs. Pollifax, hacking at his ropes. "We've not much time, you know."

"Jonesi is shielding us beautifuly from the other two, but I wish he'd stop grinning at me," complained Cyrus. "What do you suggest I do, my dear, take on Simon?"

"Oh no," gasped Mrs. Pollifax. "Amy, *please*. Just move her out of the way somehow. Oh dear, they're coming back now. Cyrus—"

"Yes, m'dear?"

"Good luck or goodbye, I don't know which, but—"

"Steady there," he said gravely, and climbed to his feet, keeping his wrists together as if they were still bound.

Mrs. Pollifax, too, arose, and stood beside the tree, her heart beating tumultuously.

"Who's next?" asked Amy, walking toward them with Simon close behind her. She came to a stop and smiled up at Cyrus.

Casually Cyrus leaned over and encircled her with his freed hands, turned her around to face Simon and held her in front of him with a viselike grip. "Well, Simon?" he said.

Simon's eyes dropped to Cyrus' wrists and one hand

moved toward his gun. Before he reached it Mrs. Pollifax stepped out from behind the tree and delivered her very best horizontal slash to the side of his throat. A look of utter astonishment passed over Simon's face, he lifted a hand toward his throat and then sank to the ground like a crumpled paper bag.

"Incredible," said Cyrus.

Amy said, "My God, what do you think you're doing?" and then she looked toward Reuben and Mainza, who had seen none of this, and began screaming.

Mrs. Pollifax snatched up Simon's rifle and called to Reuben and Mainza, "Don't touch your guns or we'll shoot!"

The two men gaped at her across the clearing, too surprised to move. Amy stopped screaming. Holding her tightly in front of him, Cyrus slowly advanced across the clearing toward the two men. Mrs. Pollifax followed with the rifle and Jonesi danced along beside her laughing.

"Feel like Jack Armstrong the all-American boy," growled Cyrus halfway across the clearing. "Damned if it isn't working too. Pick up their rifles, my dear."

"Gladly."

Amy, struggling in Cyrus' grasp, cried, "You're fiends, both of you, they could have shot me."

"Oh stop," said Mrs. Pollifax crossly, "you know very well they'd never have shot you, Amy. *I've* known it since last night when you thought I was asleep."

"Oh," gasped Amy. *"Oh!"* and a string of expletives poured out of her, followed by a number of references to barnyard animals which Mrs. Pollifax thought showed a great paucity of imagination on Amy's part.

"Amy's wrists are still tied," said Cyrus, ignoring the

stream of obscenity. "Need rope now for Reuben and Mainza, and as soon as possible, I think." Looking beyond them he called out, "Jonesi, be careful with that rifle."

Jonesi had picked up Mainza's gun before Mrs. Pollifax could reach it, and was cradling it lovingly in his arms. Hearing his name spoken, he backed away and sat down on the ground, the rifle across his knees, his face defiant.

"So long as he doesn't accidentally pull the trigger . . ."

"Let him play with it for a few minutes, we can get it later," Mrs. Pollifax told him. "We need that rope most of all."

This problem occupied them for some moments, because there was no alternative but to knot together the sections of rope they'd cut from their own wrists. It was tedious work. When Reuben and Mainza had been rendered inactive Cyrus stepped back and said in a pleased voice, "Very, very good," and then he asked, "Now what, my dear?"

Mrs. Pollifax looked at him in dismay. "Now what?" she faltered. She realized that his question exposed a dilemma that seemed too distant an hour ago to ever become real. She was confronted with the fact that Sikota was still to be anticipated, they were lost in the bush, and the sun was already very low on the horizon and withdrawing light from the savannah. It would soon be dark. "Now what?" she repeated.

"I can answer that for you, madam," said a voice behind them. "You will please drop the guns and lift your hands in the air."

They spun around in astonishment. "*Jonesi?*" gasped Mrs. Pollifax.

"Yes, madam," said Jonesi the poacher in excellent English. "You have been most helpful to me, I thank you." Bringing a small object out of his pocket he put it to his lips and blew. A piercing whistle filled the air, and from the copse of trees several hundred yards away a number of men came running. In the growing dusk it was difficult to count heads but she thought there were six or seven of them, all carrying rifles.

"Police?" gasped Mrs. Pollifax.

"Not police, no madam," said Jonesi, looking amused. "The police are in Lusaka far, far away. You are *our* captives now."

"Oh *no*," protested Mrs. Pollifax. "I thought—I hoped—"

"This," said Cyrus, blinking, "is exactly like being swallowed by a shark, who's then swallowed by a whale, who's then swallowed by a—my dear, what is the matter?"

"I'm not sure," whispered Mrs. Pollifax, staring at the men who had emerged out of the dusk and were fanning out to encircle them. One in particular among them had caught her eye, a man taller than the others, in khaki shorts, puttees, a thick sweater and a felt cavalry hat that heavily shadowed his face. Something about the way he moved. . . . He strode toward them now with a rifle slung across his shoulder, stopped to give Amy Lovecraft a long hard look, and then continued on to Jonesi.

Deep inside of her Mrs. Pollifax began to smile. The smile surfaced slowly, arriving on her lips at the same moment that the man saw her. He stopped in his tracks, appalled. "My God I'm hallucinating," he said.

"Absolutely not," she told him, tears coming to her eyes.

"But—Duchess?" he said incredulously. "Emily Pollifax from New Brunswick, New Jersey? *Here*?"

He began to laugh. "I don't believe it. Duchess, what in the name of all that's holy are you doing in the middle of Africa with this bunch of cutthroats? Or to put it more bluntly," he said, sweeping her off the ground in an exuberant hug, rifle and all, "what the hell are you up to now, Duchess?"

CHAPTER
13

When Farrell joined them some minutes later they were seated at a campfire, built for them by one of his young men. Farrell sat down, crossed his legs under him, and said, "There—business taken care of." He looked at Cyrus and then he looked at Mrs. Pollifax and he grinned. "Never saw you look better, Duchess, except for the bruise that's rapidly blossoming on your right cheekbone."

"A souvenir from Simon," said Mrs. Pollifax. "Did I hear them call you Mulika?"

"It's a name they've given me." His smile was breathtaking, a flash of white in his tanned face. She'd forgotten how handsome he was. He looked ruddy and healthy, and his mustache was infinitely more dashing than she remembered. "And by the way, Jonesi begs me to apologize to you both. He asks you to remember that you traveled in bad company and if your hands were tied, so were the hands of the other lady."

"Has a point there," admitted Cyrus.

"He found it a damn puzzling situation. Sorry, incidentally, that we've had to postpone dinner—"

"Food?" breathed Mrs. Pollifax.

"—but we're expecting Sikota, you know, which is why you've been moved out of harm's way. Now for heaven's sake, Duchess, *talk*. Tell me how in hell you and Cyrus got here, and why."

Mrs. Pollifax obligingly talked. She referred briefly to her arrival in Lusaka and then she concentrated on a description of their last twenty-four hours. When she had finished, Farrell looked stunned.

"I can't believe it," he said. "You just walked into the *Times of Zambia* office and placed an advertisement for me in the personals column?"

"It seemed very logical," she told him. "I couldn't find you."

He shook his head at her. "That directness of yours, Duchess, is going to cost you your life one of these days."

"Nearly did," said Cyrus. "Apparently."

"And you didn't even see the advertisement," lamented Mrs. Pollifax. "I thought—just for a moment, you know—that you might have come to rescue us! Farrell, what *did* bring you here in the nick of time? And why shouldn't I have advertised for you? And how do you come to be called Mulika?"

He hesitated and then he said flippantly, "Believe it or not, *mulika* means 'shedder of light' in the Nyanga language. Surprise you?" He looked at her and added soberly, "So help me I've tried to shed some, Duchess, because I've fallen in love with this country. You've heard of middle-age passion? Well, mine is directed at Africa in general—uncluttered, still unpolluted—and at Zambia in particular. Actually I came here to farm—"

"*Not* an art gallery," said Mrs. Pollifax, nodding.

"—and I do own two hundred acres in the Southern Province, but I don't see them very often these days because I've been helping train and instruct freedom fighters."

"Freedom fighters!" exclaimed Mrs. Pollifax. "So that's it . . . But surely—" She frowned over this, puzzled. "Surely that's not enough to explain Simon's abnormal interest in you? He and Amy were ready to commit murder to find out what you look like. There must be other men doing this who don't—"

"Don't have a price on their heads?" He grinned. "A pity you see that, Duchess. Yes, of course there's more, because with passion one always gets involved. You see, it's all very exciting to watch Zambia grow and develop, but next door you have Zambabwe—or Rhodesia, as you probably know it—and the people over there straggle across our border, some of them having been handled roughly, to say the least, most of them just out of prison or about to be arrested and sent off to prison, and the contrast isn't very nice. These people want autonomy too, they wither under *apartheid*—God, it's such a waste—and they need to be listened to.

"And so," he went on, his eyes gleaming in the firelight, "I got involved. With my background and my white skin I became something of a spy. You've heard of spies?" he asked, his smile mischievous. "I began traveling back and forth across the border as a fake tourist, oh-ing and ah-ing at Zambabwe's natural wonders, which are considerable, and I helped Jonesi set up a damn good underground escape route. Even lived briefly in Salisbury. Unfortunately it came to be known that a man named Mulika was guiding men out of Rhodesia, and then eventually that Mulika was a white man, and after that they learned my real name, I knew that. But your advertisement, Duchess, so direct and so naïve—" He shook his head. "It must have caused a number of tidal waves in more than a few small ponds."

"Including the Zambian police," she told him. "I was interviewed by a—oh," she gasped, "*now* I realize what was wrong with that interview. How blind of me! He didn't want to know anything about you at all, only how I came to know that you were in Zambia."

"Who?"

"A Lieutenant Dunduzu Bwanausi," she said.

Farrell burst out laughing. "Dundu? God, you must have alarmed him. I'll bet he thought you were a Rhodesian agent. I'll have to radio him all's well."

"You know him?"

"A very good friend of mine. His brother Qabaniso happens to be half owner and partner in my farm."

Their campfire was small, far removed from the burial ground, and on an incline from which they could watch a larger campfire being built some five hundred yards away. Mrs. Pollifax found her attention distracted now by Jonesi's activities. Amy Lovecraft and her confederates had been placed around the fire, their wrists still bound, and Mrs. Pollifax saw that Jonesi was tying gags across their mouths.

Following her glance Farrell said dryly, "The goats are being tethered to catch the lion, Sikota being the lion.

And a rather big one, I suspect, well worth catching."

"Rather hard on Mrs. Lovecraft, isn't it?" asked Cyrus.

"No harder than for Simon and Reuben and Mainza," pointed out Farrell, "but of course you're still laboring under the illusion that she's Amy Lovecraft, aren't you. She's not," he said, his voice hardening.

"Who is she?" asked Mrs. Pollifax.

"A Rhodesian by the name of Betty Thwaite. She's given us a hell of a time catching up with her, because from what we've been told she certainly didn't come to Zambia to abduct anyone, and the bush country is the last place we thought of looking for her."

"It's Amy you were hunting for, then?"

"Desperately," he said. "Night and day and around the clock for the past six days."

"Why?" asked Cyrus.

"Well, to give you her background, she's the intelligence behind a fanatical right-wing group in Rhodesia, one of those situations where a group takes a more extreme stance than the government, and then, like the *Herstigte Nasionale Party*, breaks away to form its own party, which in turn provokes several more spinoffs, and by this time you're deep among the fanatic fringe. That's where you find Betty Thwaite's group, all gung-ho for slaughtering anyone who suggests compromise or reason. Even the Rhodesian Government doesn't claim Betty. All we knew," he said, "was that she'd been smuggled across the border into Zambia last week, either by boat at night across the Zambesi River near Livingstone, or through the swamps into Botswana and then into Zambia. We also knew that she'd left Rhodesia with a forged Kenya passport and a change in name and in hair color, but why she decided to switch horses in midstream and kidnap you, Duchess, I just don't know. It certainly wasn't her purpose in coming here."

"But she did kidnap me!"

"Yes, and that's what baffles me," he said, scowling. "Oh I have to admit there was some sense in her madness, because if you'd given them what they wanted it would have been a real coup for her, and she's a very ambitious woman. The next time I crossed the border into Zambabwe—" He circled his throat with a finger. "Curtains."

Cyrus said, "But she didn't arrive here with that in mind?"

Farrell shook his head. "That's what's so damn puzzling. According to our informant—and he's never been wrong before—she was coming to Zambia for the purpose of assassinating President Kaunda."

"Assassinating?" said Mrs. Pollifax, suddenly alert.

"Good God," said Cyrus. "Why?"

"Why assassinate Kenneth Kaunda? Because KK, as he's affectionately called, is a gentle but insistent force against *apartheid*, Cyrus. He's been making behind-the-scene appeals to both Rhodesia and South Africa for diplomatic talks on compromise, and what's more, they've begun listening to him."

"Assassinate," repeated Mrs. Pollifax, frowning.

He nodded. "You can understand our panic. We had only an old photograph to work with, and time's been against us. We batted zero until we found a waiter at the Livingstone airport restaurant who remembered her, and that's when we learned she was a blonde, after which we linked her with the flight to Ngomo airstrip traveling as a Mrs. A. Lovecraft. She stayed a few nights at Ngomo Lodge and then flew to Lusaka, where we discovered that she arrived just in time to join—of all things—a safari party." He shook his head. "But it doesn't make sense," he said. "It simply doesn't make sense, her going off on a *safari*."

"It could," said Mrs. Pollifax softly, trying to control the excitement that had been rising in her. "It could, Farrell. It's possible that Amy Lovecraft came on safari to meet the *real* assassin."

"Meet the—*what?*" said Farrell.

"Because that's why I'm here," she told him, nodding. "I don't know about your Betty Thwaite, but I do know about assassins. It's why *I* joined the safari." She glanced pointedly at Cyrus and then back at Farrell. "I was sent," she added, "by a mutual friend of ours named Carstairs?"

"Good heavens," said Farrell, and now they both turned and looked at Cyrus, who regarded them benignly but lifted one eyebrow, waiting.

Farrell said, "Do you tell him, or shall I?"

"Tell me what? That you didn't," said Cyrus, "live next door to Emily in New Brunswick, New Jersey, or build a soapbox car for her son? Already guessed that, young man. How *did* you two meet?"

Farrell grinned. "Would you believe tied back to back in Mexico, after being doped and carried off by the—"

"Farrell!" she gasped. "You're overdoing this."

"Nonsense," said Farrell. "My dear Reed, if you're so obtuse that you believe this charming but terribly resourceful lady does nothing but raise geraniums, then you're not at all the man for her, and it strikes me from the way you look at her—"

"Farrell!" sputtered Mrs. Pollifax.

Cyrus said in his mild voice, "Certain—uh—arts have become apparent to me. A persuasive bending of truth, shall we say, and then there was the karate—"

"Karate!" It was Farrell's turn to be surprised. "Duchess, you astonish me, you're becoming a pro?"

"Pro what?" asked Cyrus quietly.

"She had this little hobby," Farrell said blithely. "As CIA courier. Sandwiched in between—if I remember correctly—her garden club and hospital activities. That's how I met her, except that three years ago I resigned from the CIA and wrote finis to that chapter. But if you don't mind assimilating this little bombshell later, Cyrus, I want very much to learn about this safari. Enlighten me, please, Duchess. And fast."

She told him all that she knew. "But Carstairs was certain enough of his informant to send me here. I was simply to take pictures of everyone on safari, nothing more, so that every member of the safari could be traced—"

She stopped as Cyrus let out an indiscreet roar of laughter. "Sorry," he said, subsiding into chuckles. "Not really amusing except—those snapshots!"

Mrs. Pollifax gave him a reproachful glance before she added, "Carstairs seemed very sure that Aristotle would be on the safari to meet someone and discuss his next project, and if Amy Lovecraft's been heavily involved in her Rhodesian group all this time I can't see her wandering around the world shooting people. I'm only assuming, of course, but putting our two stories together—"

Farrell said abruptly, "I'm going to break radio silence and call Dundu. I'm stricken by the same assumptions, Duchess, because your story fits into mine like the one missing piece of a jigsaw puzzle." He nodded. "It certainly explains why Betty Thwaite headed for a safari of all things, and if she'd already concluded her business with

Aristotle, it also explains why she could go off on a tangent and take on an abduction. She eavesdropped on your interview with Dundu and realized that one of her traveling companions was a woman who actually knew and could identify me. She couldn't resist. The abduction must have been done on impulse, and of course it was terribly unprofessional of her, but she thought she could handle both. Yes, very ambitious woman, Betty Thwaite. But I don't like using the radio, damn it."

"Why?" asked Cyrus.

"Because that's how we discovered and pinpointed *your* party," he said. "We'd left Chunga camp for Kafwala and stopped on the road to radio our whereabouts to headquarters, and that's when we overheard Simon calling Green-Bird in Lusaka. The code name Green-Bird was not unfamiliar to us," he went on, "so while we continued to Kafwala to look for Mrs. Lovecraft, Jonesi set out alone to track you down. Very good at that sort of thing, Jonesi. He wore a homing device in his cap so that we could find him again."

"As a fool, Jonesi was certainly convincing," commented Mrs. Pollifax.

"Oh God yes, he can go anywhere with that act, it's saved his life innumerable times. But Duchess, let's get back to basics: which of those people on safari do you suspect is Aristotle?"

"I've no idea," she said truthfully. "I'd say none of them, except that my first film was stolen from my room at Kafwala camp, which implies that my picture-taking bothered someone a great deal. It had to have been Aristotle who stole the film because Cyrus told me that Amy Lovecraft and Dr. Henry stayed down at the campfire while I was gone. Amy could tell you who Aristotle is, of course."

"I wouldn't bet on that," he said dryly. "So we can assume that Aristotle's still with the safari, and the assassination's already been scheduled?" He shivered. "I'm not sure that Zambia could survive as a country without President Kaunda. He's a damn strong leader and a beloved president. Any leader's a genius who can hold together a country of at least seventy different tribes speaking sixteen major languages and make it all work." He stared into the fire, frowning, and then he looked up and said sharply, "All right, this is Thursday night. Where's the safari now?"

"Camp Moshe," said Cyrus promptly. "Tomorrow they make their way back to Chunga camp, remain there over Friday night, and then end the safari in Lusaka on Saturday."

Farrell nodded. "Then I've definitely got to get a message to Dundu so the police can put everyone on safari under surveillance until they leave Zambia. Give me their names. It may save time to radio them now." He drew pencil and paper out of his pocket.

"There's Cyrus' daughter, Lisa Reed," began Mrs. Pollifax.

"And Dr. Tom Henry," added Cyrus.

Farrell looked up. "Not the chap from the mission hospital over near the Angolan border?" When Mrs. Pollifax nodded he said, "Small world. Go on."

"John Steeves, travel writer, and a very charming man. Willem Kleiber—Dutch I think he said, very prim and hygienic and in heavy construction work, whatever that means. And then there's—well, McIntosh."

Farrell stopped writing. "Yes?"

"According to Amy Lovecraft, that's only half his name. She peeked at his passport. Of course anything she said is suspect now, but I can't see any ulterior motive in her saying that unless it was true."

Farrell put down his pencil. "What sort of person is he?"

"Secretive," said Mrs. Pollifax.

Cyrus cleared his throat and said cautiously, "Reserved, in my estimation. Businessman. American."

"But always traveling," added Mrs. Pollifax.

"All right, who else?" asked Farrell.

"Chanda," said Cyrus. "Dr. Henry's protégé, who, I might add, tracked down Emily's abductors for me, and then went back to camp on foot to guide any search parties. Age twelve."

"Yes, and where are those search parties?" asked Mrs. Pollifax.

"No idea, Duchess. I'm sorry, but it's a damn big park." He gave her a rueful smile. "When you were taken west they undoubtedly went east, and now that you've headed south they're probably combing the north. That's usually the way, isn't it? Okay, we've Lisa Reed, Dr. Tom Henry, John Steeves, Willem Kleiber, the mysterious McIntosh, and young Chanda. Anyone else?"

"Amy Lovecraft, Emily and myself," said Cyrus. "Nine in all."

"Right." Farrell pocketed the memo and rose to his feet. "I'm going to radio Dundu now. Sit tight and I'll send a man over to guard you while I'm gone because this campfire has to be extinguished in a few minutes."

Mrs. Pollifax looked at him in astonishment. "Guard us? Sit tight? But surely you want me down at the campfire with Amy and the others. Sikota will be expecting to see me there. He'll count heads."

Farrell shook his head. "Too dangerous for you, Duchess."

"Dangerous!" she gasped, standing up. "Farrell, this is an assassination we're trying to stop! Of course I'm going down there."

Farrell sighed. "Look, Duchess," he said patiently, "you're tired, you need a rest. There are only seven of us men, and three are out scouting for Sikota, and anything could happen down there in the next hour."

"Absolutely right," agreed Cyrus. "Sit, Emily."

"I refuse," she told him, and grasping Farrell by the arm she turned him toward the campfire. "Look at them —four mannequins in a store window," she pointed out hotly. "No movement at all, no one talking, eating, smiling or lifting their hands. Sikota isn't a lion, he's a man with a brain that reasons. Those people abducted me and I'm missing, and then he'll wonder why nobody moves, but if Cyrus and I—"

"Ha," snorted Cyrus.

"If Cyrus and I sit with them we can talk and—and pass things around, as if we're eating, which heaven only knows I wish we *could* do, having eaten nothing all day."

Farrell turned to Cyrus. "Well, Cyrus? Damn it, I've got to send this radio message."

"Both of you absolutely right," said Cyrus judiciously. "Dangerous place to be down there. Crossfire and all that if he slips past your men." He considered this, sighed and climbed to his feet. "Have to admit Emily's right, too," he added, "and if all this helps—don't happen to have a pistol, do you?"

"Take it with my blessing," said Farrell, unbuckling a holster at his belt and handing over a gun. "Take this, too," he said, reaching into his pocket, and gave him a chocolate bar.

"Food?" gasped Mrs. Pollifax.

"Food," said Cyrus. "You go along and send your message, Farrell, we'll wander along down."

"Yes, but plain or almond?" asked Mrs. Pollifax happily.

Their move to the campfire had its ludicrous aspects; Mrs. Pollifax could see this at once. She sat down on one side of Amy Lovecraft, and Cyrus on the other side, while Amy made loud gurgling protests deep in her throat, and across the fire Simon glared at them both with bloodshot, outraged eyes. From five hundred yards away the campfire had looked brilliant but now that Mrs. Pollifax sat beside it the fire seemed astonishingly small, and the darkness around it like a black curtain. She felt exposed and horribly vulnerable.

"I believe we're here to supply motion," Cyrus reminded her. "What's the matter—second thoughts, my dear?"

"You won't," she said in a small voice, "say 'I told you so'?"

"Emily," he said with a sigh, "this is no moment to become rational. I've walked twenty miles in the bush today, helped you turn the tables on these villainous creatures, I've been captured by guerillas and am now sitting here a target ripe for any passing gunman, and do you really think—can you have the effrontery to think—I would say 'I told you so'?"

"You really are a darling, Cyrus," she said, smiling.

"Thank you. Eat your chocolate."

The moments passed slowly, each one seeming inter-

minable. She and Cyrus passed twigs and pebbles back
and forth and made flippant, imaginative conversation
with a silent Amy, and then in turn with Simon, Reuben,
and Mainza. In fact, as Mrs. Pollifax pointed out, they
behaved like idiots, to which Cyrus replied that panto-
mime had always attracted him and that he enjoyed
talking with people who couldn't answer back.

It was twenty minutes later that Mrs. Pollifax became
aware of Amy suddenly stiffening beside her. She turned
and looked at Mrs. Lovecraft and found her staring off
to the left, her eyes opened very wide and filled with
alarm. Mrs. Pollifax followed her glance and she too saw
something move: a shadow paler than the darkness of
the trees. She said in a hushed voice, "Cyrus—over there,"
and fell silent, suddenly afraid, because if this was Sikota
then he had slipped past Farrell and Jonesi and the
others without being seen. She saw the shadow pause and
then start toward them from a new angle . . . the lion
approaching the tethered goats, she thought, her throat
suddenly dry, and at that moment he seemed exactly like
a wild beast stopping to sniff the air for danger. She
guessed that he was uneasy and felt a fleeting sense of
pity for him, as if he really were a beast being drawn
into a trap, and then her pity dissipated as she recalled
that this was not a lion but Sikota, for whom everyone
talked, which meant he was a man skilled in torture. He
was entering now on the farthest reach of the firelight,
which began to give his pale shadow some substance.
Leaning forward to peer through the dusk, she saw the
outlines of a short, grotesquely fat man stuffed into a
pale business suit and carrying a long rifle under his arm.
She realized in astonishment that he must have arrived
by car—he *had* to have come by car in a suit like that,

and Jonesi and Farrell had expected him on foot. Then as he took several new steps toward the fire she lifted her eyes to his face and saw that his skin was a dingy white, with a thin mouth almost drowned in pouches of fat.

He had stopped, his hand caressing the trigger of the rifle, still half in shadow but his pale suit gleaming in the dusky light. *He knows something is wrong*, she thought, feeling her heart beat faster. There was a terrifying intelligence about his stillness, as if he was sending out tentacles to weigh and test the atmosphere. And then, as he hesitated, he did the one thing that nobody had anticipated: he called out sharply in a clear, imperative voice, "Simon?" and then, angrily, *"Simon?"*

And Simon, bound and gagged, could neither turn nor reply.

There was an uncomfortable, suspenseful moment of silence during which a hyena howled in the distance, and then abruptly Jonesi stepped out of the bush off to the right and shouted, "Drop the rifle!" From the opposite side of the clearing Farrell called, "Drop it, Sikota, you're surrounded!"

The man slowly turned toward Jonesi, and then he slowly turned toward Farrell. When he moved his action was sudden, all in one piece, and incredibly fast and graceful for a man of so much flesh. He lifted his rifle to his cheek, peered through the telescopic lens, pointed it at the campfire and pulled the trigger.

"Down!" shouted Cyrus.

Mrs. Pollifax agreed completely with this suggestion and rolled off to one side. Two other shots followed the first, but when she lifted her head she saw that it was not Sikota who had fired them. He lay crumpled on the ground, looking like a very large soft pile of laundry.

"Are you all right, Duchess?" shouted Farrell, and she heard the sound of running feet.

Mrs. Pollifax looked at Cyrus and he looked at her. He said unsteadily, "Well."

"Yes," she said, called to Farrell, "He missed," and stood up, brushing the dust from her clothes.

But Cyrus was shaking his head. "He didn't miss," he told her, pointing.

For a moment she didn't understand, and then she followed the direction of his pointing finger and gasped, "Oh no! Farrell? Jonesi?"

It was Jonesi who reached them first, and it was Jonesi who stepped carefully over Simon's feet and knelt beside Amy Lovecraft. Amy looked as if she'd grown tired of sitting upright and had laid down to sleep, but when Jonesi lifted her head there was a bullet hole in the precise center of her forehead; her eyes were sightless.

"Damn," exploded Farrell, coming up behind them, and he began swearing softly and relentlessly under his breath.

"Incredible shooting," said Cyrus, looking a little sick.

"He had a telescopic lens. He got past us somehow, you know. Damn it—both of them dead!"

"He thought she would talk, Mulika."

Cyrus snorted at this. "Couldn't have known our Amy, then."

"Perhaps he didn't," suggested Mrs. Pollifax, and turned away with tears in her eyes. "Sikota's a white man, Farrell, I saw him."

"Let's have a look," he said brusquely, and they followed him back to the crumpled body of Sikota. One of the men had turned him over and was staring down into his face.

"You know him, Patu?"

Patu nodded. "I know him, Mulika. He is the Portuguese who runs the curio shop on Cairo Road. Who would have thought he was a spy? He came in a truck, Mulika. Joshua is in the truck now, he says it has a false floor with space to hide people in it."

"So that's what he planned . . . Not exactly Betty Thwaite's type," Farrell said, staring down at the man, "but politics makes strange bedfellows." He straightened, his face grim. "But we've no time for postmortems. I've talked to Dundu by radio, and as soon as I give him the all-clear he's sending a helicopter for you both." He turned to Mrs. Pollifax and said angrily, "Dundu told me over the radio that President Kaunda's opening a new school in Lusaka on Sunday afternoon, the day after your safari ends. It's his only public appearance until August, and it's been heavily publicized."

"Oh-oh," said Cyrus.

"Yes. And if your Aristotle really exists," he said, his face hardening, "then I can't imagine his returning to Zambia at a later date when he's already here now. Sunday would have to be the day."

"Sunday?" said Mrs. Polifax in horror. "So soon?"

"It gives us forty-eight hours." He turned to look at Amy's body and sighed. "Cover her with one of the sleeping bags, Patu. In her own way—I scarcely care to admit it—she was a warrior. At least she wasn't a paid mercenary like Sikota and the rest of this unholy group."

"Lieutenant Bwanausi has the list now?" asked Cyrus.

Farrell nodded. "He has the list and he's probably circling now over Kafwala camp waiting to hear from me.

Chanda's been of enormous help to them, but unfortunately they didn't make contact with Chanda until this morning, and his information was outdated by then because you'd headed off in this direction. Incidentally, Duchess," he added, and a faint smile softened the grimness of his face, "Dundu reports they asked a ransom for you of fifty thousand *kwacha*."

"Now that's positively insulting," said Cyrus. "About thirty thousand in American dollars, isn't it?"

"Never mind, I'm alive," said Mrs. Pollifax, wrenching her gaze away from Amy's shrouded figure. Her eyes moved from the dying fire to the sky overhead, and then to the burial ground hidden by darkness, and back to the man at their feet. She said bleakly, "The helicopter will come, then, and whisk us away from all this, but what happens next, Farrell?"

He nodded. "You go back to Lusaka and wait," he told her. "Spend tomororw and Saturday recovering. Do a little sightseeing and try to forget tonight, because it's been a shock for you both. But I promise you this," he said in a hard voice. "There'll be no assassination, Duchess, and KK will safely open his school on Sunday afternoon. I'll promise you another thing, too," he added. "I'll meet you and Cyrus for lunch at your hotel on Sunday and I'll deliver to you the name and identity of Aristotle."

"Just like that?" said Cyrus.

"Just like that," promised Farrell, and turning to Patu he said, "Get me the radio now, Patu, we have a long night of work ahead."

CHAPTER

14

It was Sunday morning and Mrs. Pollifax stood outside the hotel entrance watching Dr. Henry pack his ancient Land Rover. It was already filled to the roof with cartons of medical supplies and bolts of brightly colored cloth, and Cyrus was strapping the last suitcase to the luggage rack. The two days of hedonistic pleasure that Farrell had prescribed for them had never materialized. Much of Friday had been spent at police headquarters making and signing statements, followed by a highly censored interview with a *Times of Zambia* newsman and a great deal of picture-taking. She and Cyrus had briefly shopped for souvenirs yesterday, but it had been impossible to forget what was going on behind the scenes. The safari party's return at midday, escorted by Lieutenant Bwanausi, had been a sufficient reminder, and Cyrus had not been allowed to see Lisa until late afternoon. Nor had she

been able to sleep well: her dreams were haunted by
fears that Aristotle would kill again and that the assassination, already set in motion, would somehow—in some
mysterious way—take place in spite of the police.

Lisa, standing beside Mrs. Pollifax, turned and gave her
a radiant smile. "It's all so incredible, isn't it?" she said.
"Do you think that as soon as I arrived in Zambia
something inside of me *knew*?"

"I think it's wonderful, and just right for you," Mrs.
Pollifax told her warmly.

"And to think that it hit us both the same way," Lisa
told her in an astonished voice. "And frightened us so
much we kept our distance, not trusting it. I know how
I felt . . . I sat at the campfire that first night talking to
John and thinking we were going to have a very pleasant
safari flirtation, and then I looked up and saw Tom and
I thought—I just thought, *Oh, my God.* Like that."

Listening to her, Mrs. Pollifax could almost forget—
but not quite—that in a few minutes she would be meeting Farrell. She smiled at Chanda, who was playing with
her multicolored parasol, opening it and closing it and
grinning, except that it was no longer hers because she had
given it to Chanda at breakfast. "It's a *bupe*," she'd told
him after conferring with Tom on the Bemba word for
gift. Now she asked Lisa, "Will you be married here or
in Connecticut?"

Lisa laughed. "All I know is that Tom, the scrupulous
guy, insists that I first see his hospital—and the funny
house with a tin roof we'll live in—and then we'll make
plans and I'll fly home and tell Dad."

Her father, joining them, looked at his watch and said
to Mrs. Pollifax, "Nearly time, my dear. Ten minutes to
twelve."

Lisa gave them each a curious glance. "You have a lunch date with that mysterious Mr. Farrell, haven't you. Will you tell us someday—you and Dad—what really happened to you out in the bush?"

"I'd tell you now," said Mrs. Pollifax, "except that it's not our story to tell. Not yet, at least." *Not until we've seen Farrell*, she reminded herself, and put this thought aside as Chanda came to say goodbye to her, the glorious multicolored parasol held high over his head.

"Goodbye, Chanda *nunandi*," she told him, gravely shaking his hand. "It's been a very real joy knowing you, and I hope—oh dear," she gasped, feeling a spoke of the umbrella become entangled in her hat.

Cyrus began to laugh.

"What is it?"

Cyrus and Tom surrounded her, and the umbrella was carefully disentangled from her hat. Lisa giggled. "It's that red feather," she told her. "It's sticking straight up in the air, all fifteen or twenty inches of it. You look like an Indian chief."

"Very charming Indian chief," Cyrus said, grasping her arm. "No time to mend it, either. Goodbye, Tom . . . Lisa, keep in touch."

"You too," she called after them.

Hurrying through the lobby toward the Coffee Hut, Mrs. Pollifax, aware of a surprising number of glances directed at her, said, "Cyrus, my hat—?"

"Very eye-catching," he told her truthfully. "Sets a new style. There—made it," he said, seating her at a table and taking the chair opposite her. "Nervous?"

"Of course I'm nervous," she told him, placing her sun-goggles and her purse on the table. "I've been nervous ever since Farrell telephoned to say they've arrested

Aristotle and he'd tell us about it at twelve."

"Should think you'd feel relieved, not nervous. Satisfied, happy."

"Of course I'm not being *logical*," she conceded, "but I find it so difficult to dislike people. I know they're frequently selfish or opinionated and egotistical, or dull or contrary and sometimes dishonest, but if one expects nothing from them it's astonishing how fascinating they are, and always full of surprises. You see, I liked everyone on our safari, which makes Farrell's message very worrisome. It means I can expect to be upset soon."

He said accusingly, "Couldn't possibly have liked Amy Lovecraft."

"No, but she—I do feel sorry for her, you know."

"Ha," snorted Cyrus. "Got herself into it. Who was it said 'character is destiny'?"

"But that's just it," Mrs. Pollifax told him eagerly. "Life is so much a matter of paths chosen and paths not taken, and Amy seems unerringly to have chosen all the paths that would lead to her appointment with Sikota the other night. I can't help feeling cosmic undertones, Cyrus. It's like watching *A* lead to *D*, and then to *M*, and eventually to *Z* for all of us."

"*All* of us?"

She nodded. "Yes, because six days ago at this hour Amy was still alive, and although we didn't know it, Farrell was down south looking for her, and you and I were sitting here having lunch together—"

"—and Aristotle, whoever he is, was buckling on his moneybelt?"

"Oh, I don't think so," she said earnestly. "It would be a numbered account in Switzerland, wouldn't it?"

"Whatever you say, my dear," he told her blandly,

"since you're so much more accustomed to this sort of thing than I. About that quiet life you said you lead . . . raising geraniums, was it?"

"I said that in *general* I live a very quiet life," she reminded him virtuously. "I do think there's a difference between living a quiet life and in *general* living a quiet life."

"Splitting hairs, my dear."

"Well, but—yes, I am," she admitted, giving him a dazzling smile. "And you noticed, didn't you."

"Sorry to keep you waiting," Farrell interrupted, pulling up a chair and joining them. "I'm afraid I can't stop for lunch with you, either, damn it, because I've got to head south and meet Jonesi in—" He stopped in midsentence, staring at Mrs. Pollifax. "Good God, Duchess, your hat?"

"Never mind the hat," she pleaded. "Who is Aristotle?"

"John Steeves."

"*Steeves?* Good heavens," said Cyrus.

"Now I really do feel upset," murmured Mrs. Pollifax. "I'm glad Lisa isn't hearing this. Farrell, are the police sure? Has he confessed?"

"I don't think you can expect a confession only hours after an arrest," Farrell told her, and with a glance at the hovering waiter, "Later, if you don't mind, we're not ordering yet . . . No, Steeves hasn't confessed, in fact he's refused even to give his home address or next of kin. The man's being completely unco-operative, which seems almost as incriminating as the parts of a gun and a silencer that were found in his luggage—apparently smuggled past Customs somehow—and the fact that, according to his passport, he was in France on the day that Messague was assassinated."

He hesitated, and Mrs. Pollifax said, "There's more?"

He nodded. "A notebook with scribblings in a code we've not been able to puzzle out yet, but on the last page—sorry, Duchess—a list of four names with dates: *Messague*, September fifth, which happens to be the day he was assassinated, *Malaga*, October thirtieth, and the names Hastings and O'Connell, which mean nothing to us at the moment but are being checked out. We think the last two were assassinations, too."

"Unbelievable," said Cyrus.

Farrell shrugged. "Perhaps, but would you have believed Amy Lovecraft was a Rhodesian named Betty Thwaite, or that the Duchess here was snapping pictures hoping to record an assassin's face?"

"Steeves," repeated Mrs. Pollifax, trying to assimilate this. *A room with a door marked Keep Out*, and Lisa saying, *He seems caught somehow—and terribly sad about it*. "Farrell, he had to have been blackmailed into it," she said. "There's no other explanation. Have you met him?"

Farrell looked amused. "Those sad spaniel eyes of his, you mean? I'm told women always want to mother a man who looks as if he's suffered, and perhaps he has, but I'd have to cast my vote for a troubled mind. Yes, I've met him."

"I wonder why he doesn't defend himself," she said, frowning, "although I suppose if he's Aristotle there's not much he can say. He's in prison?"

"Definitely in prison, yes, or President Kaunda wouldn't be dedicating the Moses Msonthi School at one o'clock today. Duchess, you've too soft a heart, it's time you retired too."

"It's just that he seemed genuinely fond of Lisa," she pointed out, "and it's so difficult to imagine any assassin being attracted to a woman and looking as if he cared."

"Someone," said Cyrus, "undoubtedly made the same remark about Jack the Ripper, my dear."

"Yes, but—all right," she conceded. "I'm sorry, it's probably the shock. What will happen to him now, Farrell?"

"For the moment, not a great deal," he said. "The man's safely tucked away, which is the main thing, booked for illegal possession of a weapon, and for smuggling that weapon into the country. It was all very discreetly handled after the safari ended, and now they've gained time to collect further evidence. Your McIntosh, by the way, turns out to be McIntosh Magruder—I thought that might interest you."

"The billionaire recluse?" said Mrs. Pollifax, startled.

"*Multi*billionaire recluse."

"Thought he never came out of seclusion," said Cyrus.

"Apparently even the Magruders of this world listen to their doctor. Magruder had been ill and his doctor advised some travel and a change of scenery. That's who McIntosh is, while Willem Kleiber jets around the world selling earthmoving machinery to developing countries."

"Very appropriate for a man who is anything but earth-shaking," commented Cyrus.

"Yes. Prim little man, isn't he? Duchess, have you been in touch with Carstairs since you came out of the bush?"

She shook her head. "It costs twelve dollars to call the United States for three minutes," she told him. "I asked. So I thought I'd wait until I could present him with Aristotle's identity, which I *think*," she added, "he'd find well worth a twelve-dollar call."

"Frugal to the end," said Farrell, "except for those hats of yours. Duchess, what happened?" He stared fascinated at the feather that shot into the air like an antenna.

"Sorry you mentioned it," Cyrus said in his mild voice. "Been trying not to notice it myself."

"I had a small accident with a parasol," she explained with dignity, "and I will presently find a safety pin and tie the feather down, since it's the only real hat I brought. Farrell, do you think Carstairs will have heard about our abduction?"

He smiled. "Don't sound so wistful, Duchess, I doubt it. You were in and out of the bush too fast to reach the American papers. Front-page news here, though. I can't help noticing how the waiters are staring at you. Unless, of course, it's the hat." He glanced at his watch and sighed. "Duchess, I loathe goodbyes, but there's this long drive ahead of me—"

"I know," she said, nodding. "We've scarcely had time to talk, but I can't complain when you and Jonesi saved our lives."

"I owed you that, you know. It makes us even," he told her with his quick smile. "Duchess, you'll have to come back to Zambia soon. With Cyrus, perhaps, to visit Lisa? Only, for heaven's sake don't advertise for me in the newspaper next time, Duchess, or it'll cost me my head. You can always reach me in care of Qabaniso Bwa-nausi at our farm, I've written down the address for you." He opened her purse and slipped a piece of paper inside, and then he pushed back his chair and stood up. "Good-bye, Cyrus, I certainly like your style . . . As for you, Duchess, one of these days—oh to hell with it, I'll just give you a quick kiss, a God bless and go."

He leaned over and hugged her, and with a nod and a wave to Cyrus he walked away.

"Oh—Farrell!" called Mrs. Pollifax after him.

He turned. "Yes?"

"I was to ask you very formally and very officially if you'd like to return to your old job. Carstairs misses you."

He grinned. "I'll take care of that myself, Duchess. Same cable address?"

"Same cable address."

He waved and walked out, and Cyrus said, "Damn decent chap, your Farrell, even if he doesn't know a soapbox derby from a horse race."

"Yes," she said, blowing her nose, and then she gave him a distracted smile and said, "Cyrus, would you mind terribly if we don't have lunch now? I think I've lost my appetite."

"I don't wonder," he said, helping her up from her chair. "A walk should do us both good."

"Thank you. I can't say that I even arrived with an appetite," she told him as they walked out of the restaurant into the lobby of the hotel. "The suspense made me edgy all morning, and now I simply can't eat when John Steeves—when he—and then Farrell going, too—"

"Perfectly understandable," he said.

He steered her through a crowd of people waiting for the elevator and came to a stop as the door of a descending elevator slid open and discharged a fresh crowd of people into the lobby. They stood patiently while the two groups exchanged places, the one swarming into the elevator, the other pushing their way through. Once in motion again, she and Cyrus fell into step behind a tall man in a turban who was hurrying toward the hotel exit. Just to one side of him walked a shorter man whose erect posture caught Mrs. Pollifax's eye next, and she transferred her gaze to him. There was something very familiar about that walk, she decided, and then she

thought, *Of course—a strut with a stutter.* She said to
Cyrus, smiling, "That's Mr. Kleiber ahead of us, Cyrus,
let's catch up with him and ask—"

She stiffened as the man glanced off to the right and
she saw his face. It wasn't Mr. Kleiber, it was a black
man wearing gold-rimmed spectacles, and so it couldn't
be Mr. Kleiber, and yet—and yet it *was* Mr. Kleiber, she
realized in astonishment, recognizing his nose and forehead, except that it was a Willem Kleiber without a
goatee and changed, somehow, into a Zambian. She saw
him walk through the glass doors and signal to a taxi and
she gasped, "Cyrus, it *is* Kleiber—run!" and breaking free
she raced after him.

"Taxi!" she cried as Mr. Kleiber drove away. A second
taxi slid up to her, she fumbled with the door, jumped
inside and gasped, "Please—follow the car that just
pulled away. Hurry!"

The taxi shot ahead just as Cyrus reached the curb.
Through the open window Mrs. Pollifax shouted to him,
"Call Dundu—call someone! Help!"

CHAPTER

15

Cyrus, suddenly bereft of his lunch partner, stared after the vanishing taxi in horror. One moment Mrs. Pollifax had been with him, and the next not. He'd distinctly heard her say, "Cyrus, that's Mr. Kleiber ahead of us," and then the man had turned his head and revealed a gleaming black Zambian face, and obviously the man wasn't Kleiber at all. But Emily had gasped, "It *is* Kleiber—run," and had left his side with the speed of a gazelle and now she was gone, heaven only knew where, shouting something about Dundu and help.

He walked back into the lobby and sat down, mourning the slowness of his reflexes and reminding himself that six days with Emily Pollifax should have proven to him that he had to be on his toes every minute. No slides, he thought, grateful for this, but instead a woman who gave sudden shouts and vanished. He wished fervently that he'd reached the taxi in time to go with her.

Again he wondered why she'd jumped into that taxi, because there had to be a reason for it. What *would* Kleiber be doing wearing gold-rimmed spectacles, a charcoal pin-striped suit and a black skin? He supposed that some sort of dye could be injected into the veins, or perhaps there were pills for that sort of thing, but the idea was insane. Still, Emily had believed it was Kleiber. Possibly she was overwrought after hearing the news about Steeves, but Emily, he decided, wouldn't be overwrought. If nearly being killed by Amy and Simon hadn't done the trick, he really didn't suppose anything could. And of course she knew now that Steeves was Aristotle, so why—?

He sat considering this until he felt a chill run down his spine, and then race up again, and when it hit the base of his skull he rose and walked over to the desk. "Look here," he said, "I want to put in a call to the police."

"Something wrong, sir?"

"Don't know but I want to call the police."

"This way, sir." The desk clerk led him into a private office and pointed to a telephone on the desk. "There you are, sir. Ring the operator and she'll connect you."

A moment later Cyrus was struggling to pronounce a name which he'd never seen spelled, and had only heard in passing. "A Lieutenant Dundu Bonozzi," he said. "Have to speak to him right away."

"Sorry sir, he's not here," said the man at the other end of the line.

"Could be a matter of life and death," Cyrus told him, feeling damnably awkward at saying such a thing. "Any way of contacting him?"

"He's at the Moses Msonthi School—guard detail, sir.

You can leave a message and we'll try to get it to him if he phones in."

"Yes," said Cyrus, feeling this was reasonable and at the same time trying to think of a way to express his unease. "All right, let's try this one. Ready?"

"Ready, sir."

"Here we are: 'Are you certain you have the right Aristotle? Kleiber left hotel as black man, Mrs. Pollifax in pursuit.'"

"A very odd message, sir."

"Indeed it is," said Cyrus uncomfortably. "Look here, anybody else there I can speak to?" But even as he said this he realized how entangled he could become in trying to explain a European in blackface to a stranger; Dundu was the only person who would understand. "Never mind," he said, "what's the name of that school again?"

"The Moses Msonthi School, sir. Manchichi Road."

"Right. I'll look for him there."

He hurried out to the entrance to find that, perversely, there were no taxis now. He paced and fumed, considered the state of his blood pressure and consulted his watch: it was 12:40 and Farrell had said the dedication ceremonies began at one o'clock . . . When a taxi finally arrived it was 12:45 and he was too grateful to express his sense of aggrievement. He climbed in and directed the driver to the school.

"Oh yes, sir, yes, sir," the driver said with a big smile. "Our president opens the school today. Very nice, very beautiful school for girls."

"Yes . . . well, see if you can get me there fast," he told him, and tried to think of what he'd do when he reached the school. There'd be crowds, he supposed; a big event opening a new school, probably speeches, perhaps not, but certainly crowds. He hadn't the slightest idea how he'd find Dundu, or whether Emily would turn up there too. Perhaps by now she'd discovered the man was a bona fide Zambian, except that if it really was Kleiber . . . Better not think about that, he decided, and practiced taking deep breaths to remain calm. The streets were relatively empty of traffic since it was Sunday and the shops were closed, but as they neared Manchichi Road the traffic increased. Cyrus paid off the driver a block away from the school and set out to find Dundu Bwanausi, not even certain that he'd mastered the man's name yet.

Mrs. Pollifax sat on the edge of her seat watching the taxi ahead and contributing frequent comments to spur the driver on. "He's wanted by the police," she confided, feeling that some explanation was becoming necessary and hoping that what she said was true but hoping at the same time that it wasn't. "Not too close, driver, we mustn't be noticed. Have you any idea where they're heading?"

"We are very near Manchichi Road, madam, perhaps he goes to watch our President dedicate a school."

Oh God, she thought, and said aloud, "Do you mean the Moses Msonthi School?"

"Yes, madam. This is Manchichi Road we turn into now, and the taxi ahead is going to the school, see? It stops now."

She began fumbling in her purse for money. "I'll get out now, I hope this is enough," she said, thrusting *kwacha* notes on him, and as he drew up to the curb she added, "But will you do something important for me, driver? Will you call the police and tell them—tell them Aristotle is at the Msonthi School? *Aristotle*."

"Aristotle. Yes, madam." He gave her a curious glance.

She climbed out and gave him a long, earnest look. "I'm depending on you, I'm depending *desperately* on you."

"Yes, madam."

Up ahead she saw Mr. Kleiber strolling around the edge of the crowd looking for a place to enter it. She hurried toward him, mentally rehearsing what possible karate blow might fell him before he could shoot President Kaunda, because of course that had to be the only reason he was here in his masquerade, which meant that her instincts about John Steeves had proven sound after all, except that Steeves was now in prison and here was Aristotle still free, and no one knew . . .

It was frightening.

The sun was glittering, and shone on women in colorful blouses and skirts with babies slung over their shoulders, on barefooted children and men in overalls and in solemn Sunday best. A very neat avenue had been left clear for the President, she noticed. She saw Kleiber examine it and then, before she could reach him, he slipped into the crowd and vanished from sight.

Lieutenant Bwanausi was idling near a police car at the southern corner of the crowd, waiting to see his President, whose photograph hung on every wall of his small home. One of his friends passed and called out a greeting, and then came over and shook hands with him, asking how things went with him. Dundu thought back on his week's work, recalled how close an assassin had come to threatening the life of his President, and said that life went very well for him indeed. His friend strolled on, and hearing the crackle of static from the car radio behind him, Dundu reached for the microphone. "Bwa-nausi here."

At first he didn't understand what Soko was saying. "How is this, your speaking the name Aristotle, Soko," he said. "Two messages?"

First, it seemed, there had been the message from a man at the Hotel Intercontinental, which Soko now read to him. "But Dundu," he protested, "I thought the man was drunk. Now a second call has come in from a taxi driver. He says he and a woman chased a taxi to Man-chichi Road, and this woman pleaded with him to call us and say that Aristotle is at the school."

Dundu felt a spasm of fear. Was this possible? Could John Steeves not be Aristotle after all? Yet how could this be, given the evidence? "Man, this is bad news," he told Soko. "Is it too late to reach KK's party? Aristotle is the code name of the assassin we thought we jailed last night."

There was a stunned silence. "Oh God," said Soko. "I'll try, Dundu, I'll try."

"Do that, send out a—" He stopped as he heard the sirens. "Too late, the President's here, Soko." He dropped the microphone and began running . . .

Mrs. Pollifax pushed her way through the crowd trying to find Mr. Kleiber, but now in her panic everybody had begun to look like Mr. Kleiber and she couldn't distinguish one face from the next. She stopped and forced herself to be calm, and instead of elbowing her way deeper into the crowd she turned and pushed her way toward the avenue down which the President would walk. Reaching the front row, she thanked a man who had let her pass and leaned out to look down the avenue. One glance was enough: she saw the President climbing out of a limousine and shaking hands with a number of people grouped around the car. She turned her head and looked to her left and saw Kleiber standing in line only twenty feet away from her, one hand in his pocket, a faint smile on his lips, his face remote, almost dreaming. Mrs. Pollifax turned and began to struggle toward him.

Cyrus had given up trying to find Lieutenant Bwanausi. He had withdrawn to a playground behind the crowd and had climbed to the top of a convenient jungle gym, from which he could sit and keep an eye out for a familiar face. He held little hope of finding one now, and if he didn't he wondered if Emily would expect him to throw himself across the President's path. Probably, he thought, and hearing a sudden ripple of cheers from off to his right, he realized that it was one o'clock and that President Kaunda must have arrived and that he'd better do something. Before climbing down he took one last look at the knots and clusters of people on the fringe of the crowd, framed against the wall of heads beyond, and then he realized that for several minutes he'd been absently watching something—a red stick or a pennant—move determinedly from a point on his right toward an unknown point on his left. Staring at it intently now, his eyes narrowing, it stirred his memory.

Emily's feather, he thought in astonishment, and taking a quick fix on it he climbed down from his jungle gym and hurried to the edge of the crowd, entered it at some distance ahead of where he judged Emily to be, and alternately pushed and shoved his way inward. He was in luck: the first time he stopped to look for the feather he spotted it some twenty feet away. Assuming that Emily was under

it, he moved forward to intercept her, and at that moment
the crowd shifted and he saw her. He also saw, not far
away from her, the back of a man wearing a charcoal
pin-striped suit: Kleiber.

Emily had seen Kleiber too. She crept forward, the
feather at a ridiculous slant now, and when she moved in
beside the man, Cyrus, thrusting aside several small children to reach her, guessed what she was planning to do.
She had just lifted her right hand when Kleiber turned his
head and looked at her. Cyrus saw them exchange a long
glance, and then he saw the gun in Kleiber's hand and he
caught his breath, appalled. Slowly Kleiber lifted the gun
and pointed it at Mrs. Pollifax, who froze, staring at him
in astonishment.

Cyrus gasped, "*Not* karate, Emily—judo now." Mem-
ories of long-ago gymnasium classes came back to him,
of a dreary evening spent in throwing and being thrown
to the mat, and with only a fleeting thought to brittle
bones, Cyrus hurled himself across the twelve feet of
space that separated them. His shoulders met solid flesh,
there was a crunch of bone meeting bone, several sharp
cries, and he and Emily Pollifax, Willem Kleiber and two
small boys fell to the ground together.

Only Dundu Bwanausi, racing to them from the opposite side, knew that five people had not been accidentally
pushed to the ground by the crowd. He leaned over
Kleiber with a grim face, pocketed the man's gun and
snapped handcuffs on his wrists. He picked up the two
crying children and dusted them off. He gave Cyrus a
hand, and then he helped Mrs. Pollifax to her feet and
carefully restored her hat to her. Only when he looked
into her face did his expression change. He said softly,

fervently, "Oh madam, *zikomo—zikomo kuambeia,* ten thousand times *zikomo* . . ."

But Cyrus, too, had something to say. "Damn it, Emily," he complained, "only way to keep an eye on you is marry you. Think we could find a quiet corner and talk about that?"

CHAPTER
16

In Langley, Virginia, it was Monday morning and Carstairs, returning from an early conference Upstairs, was scowling.

"Something wrong?" asked Bishop, looking at him curiously. "Or wronger than usual?"

Carstairs poured himself a cup of coffee before answering. "Not really," he said, "except that my ego's suffered a small blow."

"Oh?"

Carstairs made a face. "You know I've never enjoyed being outmaneuvered by the British . . . Upstairs asked for a review of the Aristotle file this morning, and damned if Liaison didn't report that British Intelligence has a man on Aristotle's trail too."

Bishop began to understand. He said with a grin, "You mean one of Emily's safari companions was an M1 agent?"

Carstairs nodded. "Some travel writer or other. Seems a damned waste of talent."

Bishop chuckled. "Think he was taking snapshots too?" He had a sudden vivid picture of Mrs. Pollifax and a British agent swarming over the safari with their cameras.

"It's no longer important," Carstairs said, shrugging. "The safari ended Saturday and we'll soon have Mrs. Pollifax's photographs, and we can pool the results with London and Interpol. The pictures are what matter, although I'm certainly hoping she'll bring us Farrell as a dividend. I wonder if they've had their reunion yet . . ."

"As a matter of fact they have, sir."

Carstairs put down his cup of coffee and stared. "You've heard from her?"

"No," said Bishop, "but this cable arrived from Zambia while you were in conference. It's from John Sebastian himself, no less, datelined 2 P.M. yesterday Zambian time."

Carstairs brightened. "Marvelous! Is he coming back to us?"

"No," said Bishop, and read aloud:

SORRY CHAPS BOOKED SOLID FOR NEXT FEW YEARS STOP SUGGEST YOU BOOK EMILY HOWEVER BEFORE CYRUS BEATS YOU TO IT STOP DELIGHTED TO FIND DUCHESS STILL INDESTRUCTIBLE ALTHOUGH NOT FOR WANT OF TRYING STOP RETURNING HER TO YOU ONLY SLIGHTLY BRUISED WITH LOVE AND KISSES FARRELL.

"Now what," said Carstairs, "is that all about?"

"I suspect he'd been drinking, sir," said Bishop, and tossed the cable into the wastebasket.